# WALKING ALONE W
## PARANORMA
### INTRODUCTIC

I was born in the late 1960s, the youngest child of five kids, with two older brothers and sisters. The plus side of being the youngest was that my parents spoiled me, because I was the baby.

The downside, however, was that everything I got, whether it was clothes or toys, were hand-me-downs. I rarely had anything new to call my own.

My dad was a man of his times; a hard-worker and a good provider for the family. He showed me the value of a work ethic and taught me that a person has to work for what they want. No one slacked off in our household. Everyone had their jobs and were expected to do them to the best of their ability. That work ethic he instilled in me still drives and shapes me to this very day.

Though my dad was the force that pushed me along in life, my mom has truly been my inspiration. Even though she balanced raising the kids, as well as dealing with her own personal hardships, she still maintained a positive outlook on her life and the lives of her children. A devout Catholic, she has a rock-solid faith in God, prays the Rosary daily and refuses to give up hope, even when the days are the darkest. If I took my work ethic from my father, my mother gave me her strong sense of faith.

Growing up in the '70s was the best time to be alive. By the time I was six, I knew what I wanted to be in life; I wanted to be a police officer. When I was in kindergarten, I proudly carried my "Adam-12" lunchbox to school. You know the one? The metal one with a cool thermos inside? While other little girls had "Buffy and Jodi" from Family Affair, I had Reed and Malloy to protect my peanut butter and jelly!

My days were filled with eating a quick breakfast and then spending the rest of the day playing outside with my friends. Freeze-Tag, Kick the Can, Cops and Robbers and riding our bikes filled our mornings and afternoons. Long before kids spend their days sitting in air conditioning playing video games and watching YouTube, we sweated in the sunlight, only taking breaks to drink from a hot hosepipe in the front yard. And if you were inside for an extended period, it meant that you had been grounded and sent to your room.

For a child of ten, this was tantamount to a life sentence or hard labor on The Rock. All you wanted was to be outside, running and playing with your friends, until the streetlights came on, signaling that it was time to go home.

But then, things took a more serious, and drastic change once I entered high school.

In one year alone, I lost five friends. Some to natural causes, others to suicide. The onslaught of grief threw me into a downward spiral, causing me to experience panic attacks before I even knew what they were.

There were no "Grief Counselors," or "Safe Spaces" that I could confide or hide in. I forced myself to bury my feelings and put a fake smile on my face, to fit in. While the normal kids were having the times of their lives in sports, yearbook committee, and student counsel, I walked the hallway, all the while wanting to find a corner to crawl into and cry.

At one point, I lost so much weight that the doctor told my mother that I needed to be admitted to the hospital. So, at sixteen, I was on medication for my stomach just to keep food down, and antidepressants to keep my mood up.

I was a basket case.

During this time, I was also working at McDonald's. And keeping with my work ethic, I showed up on time, made the burgers and smiled as I handed the happy families their happy meals, all the while wanting nothing better than to lock myself in my room and cry. And one day, just when I thought things couldn't get any worse, a classmate came into the restaurant, and in a laughing voice, told me that a close personal friend of mine, another girl of sixteen, had died of a seizure.

This girl, who very easily could have been me, had died, and the way my classmate decided to tell me was by laughing at it! I was horrified at the nonchalant way she relayed the information to me.

The parallels to my own life were shocking. My friend was the same age, appeared to be perfectly healthy, and she just died. The breath caught in my throat.

"Is that going to happen to me?"

I felt a chill, as if the Grim Reaper himself had his hand on my heart, weighing and measuring me, to see if I was worthy of the life I had.

The thought of the power and sway that Death had over a person terrified me. If the very young were not immune to His clutches, then how could I escape the inevitable?

So, I decided to beat Death at its own game. I would decide when I would die on my own terms, and not his. (I know that kind of thinking is ridiculous, but between the depression and the medication, that was how messed up I was).

I tried to keep my intentions from my family and friends, but my mom knew. I wouldn't find that little bit of information until I was in my forties and she and I were having a heart to heart one day. Mom told me, "I was always afraid that I would come home and find you dead from suicide."

This crushed me. I finally came clean and told her that I had tried to overdose on pills and then told her that I had dropped the bottle in the toilet to explain the loss of ninety pills. But apparently, I couldn't even kill myself right, because the pills didn't do their job and I never tried anything like that again.

After surviving my teen years, I began to understand things that before made no sense to me at all. It was like one giant puzzle that finally started to come together, so that I could see the big picture.

In 1987, I was nineteen and met my future husband. And as all great love stories go, I met him in a bar. Cliché'? yeah, but life can be like that.

I saw him on the dance floor with his friends, and in my nineteen-year-old mind I thought, "He wouldn't give me the time of day."

He danced the night away, while my unpopular and basket-case self, simply stood back and watched.

Every weekend, my friends and I would go back to that bar just to watch him dance. This didn't sit too well with my girlfriends, (and truth be told, if you asked him, he'd tell you that I was stalking him, but that is up to the courts to decide and the statute of limitations have long since expired). And then one day, he did notice me.

And he asked me out.

We started dating and I didn't want him to know I was on medication, so I threw it out. And thanks to the love of this man, I never went back.

After six months, we decided that we would get married. We decided to elope, avoiding the wrath of the nay-sayers who said that we hadn't known each other long enough and were taking bets that it wouldn't last.

After thirty-three years, we are still married and doing fine. The only difficulty that we have encountered is collecting all that money from the bets made against us.

In 1990, our first child was born. Since any first birth is an adjustment to new parents, we dealt with the challenges of raising a newborn. Normal things like two AM feeding, changing diapers and digging applesauce out of the rug were a day-to-day occurrence, but experiencing "paranormal" incidents isn't normally covered in your everyday "What to expect from an infant," handbook.

And when I say paranormal, I'm not talking about the run-of-the-mill "Mom, there's a monster under my bed" sort of thing.

I mean "Give Linda Blair a run for her money," sort of encounters that carried over later in my life.

This was where it first started…or was it?

In the late '90s, I told my husband that I wanted to pursue my dream of becoming a police officer. Since the children, (we had our second one by this time) were older, I felt that it was the perfect time to accept my calling as a protector. But it wasn't easy. After applying five times, I was finally accepted and attended the police academy. This was a scary time for me since I had been with McDonald's for eighteen years. And I was uncertain what the future would bring.

In 2002, after six months in the academy, my dream finally came true.

I was a Police Officer.

I spent my first six years working uniform patrol, but my eyes were set on another dream; I wanted Crime Scene. When I wasn't stopping vehicles or handling domestic disputes, I read everything I could get my hands on about forensics, developing fingerprints and collecting evidence. I spent a day with one of the top crime scene detectives on the force, who awarded my work with my own fingerprint kit. And the work paid off. After processing my own scenes and getting back numerous positive hits on the prints I submitted, the techs in the lab began to notice my work. I decided to apply for the first Criminalist position that opened in our Homicide Division.

This girl, who was so terrified of death just a few years earlier, was now applying for a position in the unit who dealt with death on a daily basis, up close and personal.

The irony was not lost on me.

And, to my own amazement, I was awarded the job, even with the little bit of experience I had. Thirteen years later, I am still working Homicide and the fears and trepidation of that sixteen-year-old girl have fallen to the wayside.

As I mentioned, back in the '90s when my son was born, we began to experience paranormal events. These experiences continued to plague and fascinate in some profound, scary, and often inspirational ways.

So, sit back and get comfortable. The journey into the unknown is beginning.

## Chapter One

## The Beginning

For me, this is my first memory that messages were somehow coming to me in my dreams. Although back then, I didn't know this was a message.

When I decided I was going to write this book, I was discussing with my mom this particular dream, because I wasn't sure how old I was when this event happened. After discussing it, we narrowed it down, I was between the ages of 6 and 10 years old.

I can remember a dream that I had hundreds of times, but I didn't know what it meant when I was very young. There wasn't much to the dream, actually, it was more like a clip of a movie that played over and over again. It's weird, I can still see the dream just as vivid now as the very first time I had it.

So here it is. Are you ready?

I dreamt that there was a very young Angel, maybe 8 yrs. old, glowing, beautiful and floating above the top of the stairs by my bedroom. That's it! I know you were ready for some long-drawn-out dream, but that's all she wrote. It played over and over and over again. Hundreds of times.

It wasn't until I was compiling my stories for this book that it "clicked" on what this dream meant. I don't know why it never did before then, but it just didn't.

So, the event I spoke of earlier was when I was between the ages of 6 and 10 years old. My two older brothers and two older sisters and I were playing "Rock Monster!" This was in the early 70's well before electronics and video games, so you came up with the craziest names for the games we played.

Ok, so the game is played like this, the person who is it puts a sleeping bag over their head and you have to find one of the other four hiding in one of the three rooms in our upstairs. You have to stay put until you are found, no moving around, you just stay put until they find you. The first one found is then it, the monster. Now, the upstairs at our house consisted of the boy's room, the biggest room in the house, of course, the girl's room, which was the smallest room in the house that the three of us girls had to share, and the bathroom right smack at the top of the steps. I still don't think that was fair that us girls had the smallest room and Mom still has to hear about it occasionally. Anyway, I always got into my part. It was my turn and I was the dreaded Rock Monster. I was sporting my Strawberry Shortcake sleeping bag over my head and I was moaning like I think a Rock Monster should moan and growl with my arms above my head, waddling back and forth. Now mind you, my mom and dad were downstairs at the bottom of the steps, playing cards with some friends of theirs. So, I'm walking from the girl's bedroom into the hallway when my left foot went over the edge of the top step and I went tumbling down a flight of steps. I hit the bottom landing and the way I landed everyone thought I was dead. But in true Rock Monster fashion, I jumped up, sleeping bag still partly over my head and body, raised my hands and started growling as if nothing had happened.

After this incident, I never had that dream again. Then, it dawned on me a week before I started writing this book, that I was given a message. To me, the message was a warning that I was going to fall down the steps and I was going to be okay, now looking back at it. After all, in the dream, I was on the landing looking up at angel on the top of the steps.

So, my question is, can we have dreams that are warnings or premonitions of things to come? I'm no expert by all means, but this would be the very first dream that I can remember where I feel I was given a sign that something was going to happen to me on those steps that night. This would be the first of many dreams I would encounter throughout my life.

## Chapter Two

## The First Shadow Man

When my husband Patrick and I got married in 1987, we eloped, by the way, since no one thought it was a good idea that we got married after only knowing each other a few short months, but that's another story.

We were married for a couple of years before we went on our honeymoon to Cancun, Mexico. This is where our firstborn was conceived. Sorry, too much information.

Anyway, when he was born, that's when things would change for us. This is where our paranormal experiences started.

When my son was about 6 months old, my husband and I were getting ready to go out with his cousin, to a bar no less, when I was struck with a horrible migraine.

So, we cancelled the sitter and I lay down on the bed to try and get rid of this migraine. Once my medicine kicked in, I was out.

Our son was sleeping, and my husband Patrick was in the living room. Patrick walked out of the kitchen to the living room when he thought he saw me, walking across the hallway from the bathroom to the bedroom. He came into the bedroom to check on me, shaking my leg and waking me up, which I wasn't happy about at the time.

He said to me, "Were you just in the bathroom?" in which I replied angrily, "NO! I was sleeping trying to get rid of this migraine!!" The next thing I know I hear the front door shut. He left in a hurry.

The next morning, he told me that he saw a dark figure walk from the bathroom to the bedroom where I was. He said it didn't look like me, it looked like a man, but when he checked our bedroom of the tiny two-bedroom apartment we were renting, no one was there. So, he thought it HAD to be me. When he realized he woke me up from a deep sleep and the person had vanished, he freaked out and left.

Thanks for that by the way.

Little did we know, this would be the first of MANY shadow figures in our life.

This would be just the beginning.

## Chapter Three

## Night Terrors?

When our son, Zian, was just a little over a year old he would get up in the middle of the night and scream like he was being murdered in his room. Now we are still in the same apartment where my husband Patrick saw his first shadow figure, which we had buried in the back of our minds at this point.

These night terrors, as our doctor would later call them, continued for a couple of years until he was old enough to verbalize what he was seeing, and because of these terrors we switched him from a crib to a playpen so he wouldn't hurt himself. He would scream almost every night like clockwork, 3:30 a.m.! Every. Single. Night. It was exhausting.

The Doctor told us to just let him scream through them, that he would eventually wear himself out and fall asleep. Well, we lived in a tiny two-bedroom apartment, and letting him scream bloody murder like we were beating him wasn't going to cut it. I'm still surprised to this day no one ever called the police on us. We were told he would outgrow these, and it wouldn't last long. Just be patient, they said!

When you would go into his room, he would look right through you, like you weren't even there. Thinking about it to this day still creeps me out. His eyes would be wide open, as wide as they could be, screaming and pointing to the corner of his room. It would make the hair on the back of our necks stand, because there was nothing there, not that we could see anyway. We were told not to wake him because this could startle him. Well, I was never good at following doctor's orders and would take him out of his bed and rock him until he fell asleep and slip him back into his bed and try to catch a few hours of shut-eye before my shift at work.

Well, eventually he would outgrow the screaming like he was being beaten, to screaming "There's a Monster in my room!" Now we all heard our children say this at one time or another right?! I mean, I can remember when I was little, I wouldn't let my arm or leg hang over the bed in fear the boogie man would grab me and drag me under the bed. Or I would grab the light switch in my bedroom, stretch as far as I could to my bed and then flip the switch and run and dive to my bed. Sometimes I failed miserably and missed the switch and ran to my bed and realized the light was still on! So, for the most part, we would brush this off as him being scared of the boogie man and everything else that goes bump in the night.

    By the time he was three, we would realize that Zian could see things that we couldn't. We weren't sure of what those "things" were, but we would find out in due time.

## Chapter Four

## There's a Lady in My Room

Now, this is where things get VERY interesting. We moved to a rental house; we'll call it the Oakland house. I remember when we were looking at the house with the landlord there was just one item of furniture still in the house. She told me it belonged to the previous homeowner and asked if we wanted it, otherwise, it was going in the garbage. It was too beautiful to put in the garbage, so of course I wanted to keep it.

My grandmother's China would look beautiful in it.

The house was perfect for our family that was just starting to grow. We moved there when Zian was about a year and a half and it was a cute cape cod, with two bedrooms, two bathrooms, a nice unfinished basement and a fenced-in backyard for Zian to play.

Heck, we even got a dog, Roxy.

We decided to put Zian's bedroom upstairs, because it was a large room for a little boy with a big imagination. He was so excited about his new room.

Everything seemed perfect for the first six months or so, until he started coming downstairs every night at, you guessed it, 3:30 in the morning.

This was different from his night terrors, he was a little over two years old now, he could verbalize things a little better, and let me tell you, that boy could talk like no other. He must have got that from his daddy.

By this time, I was pregnant with our daughter. I needed my sleep now more than ever, but the 3:30 wake up calls would come again. He would come downstairs and just stand at the side of our bed, staring at me. At first, he would wake me and say there was a monster in his room. I would quickly wake up Patrick and he would take him back upstairs, open the closet doors, check all of the nooks and crannies to assure Zian there weren't any monsters up there. Sometimes it worked and other times he ended up in bed with us.

This went on for a while until Patrick and I would start to see and hear things for ourselves.

There would be times, just the three of us sitting watching TV, when we would see a shadow go across the floor, coming from the kitchen.

I remember one night in particular, we were watching the Simpsons, that's right, the Simpsons (I never claimed we ever won the parents of the year award) when we saw a shadow glide across the floor.

I'm guessing shows like this gave our son the plentiful sense of humor he has to this day.

Patrick would then jump up quickly and run into the kitchen, and no one would be there. Then you start to think our minds are playing tricks on us, but we ALL saw it!

Then it starts to become a daily and nightly occurrence, if it's not shadows, it's voices, footsteps and knocks on the wall. Our dog, Roxy, would bark at the corners of the house and she would growl at the bottom landing to the upstairs hallway leading to Zian's room.

We would hear someone walking up and down the upstairs steps, and sometimes it would sound like someone was tumbling down them. Pots and pans would make noises in my cabinets but when we went into the kitchen everything was in place.

The sounds of Zian's electronic toys coming on in his bedroom, (the same toys that we had taken the batteries out of so we wouldn't have to hear them in the middle of the night) would be terrifying.

Three months into my pregnancy I started to have complications and was homebound, I had to take maternity leave extra early from work.

Now that I was home and Zian wasn't at the sitters, I started to experience more than I bargained for.

I remember taking the laundry downstairs to the basement, which by the way, used to always make the hair on my neck stand up.

I didn't like the basement AT ALL. It reminded me of the Red Room in Amityville Horror.

Anyway, I was halfway down the steps when I heard the dryer going. It sounded like a pair of gym shoes was clanking around in it. I was terrified, but somehow worked up the courage to go down and check it out.

This is usually the part where I'm yelling at the TV when I'm watching a scary movie, screaming; "DON'T GO DOWN THERE, YOU IDIOT!!!" Yet here I am going down to investigate.

I wasn't even a cop yet; I was working as an Assistant Manager at Mc Donald's. I had no business going down there.

So, I get to the bottom of the steps and the dryer stops. I see the cord is flung over the top of it, not even plugged in.

That was it for me, I didn't even check to see if it was warm. I ran up those steps as fast as a pregnant girl could run, (and believe me, this pregnant girl could put Usain Bolt to shame) I slammed the door and locked it.

What made matters worse, is that the basement steps were the see-through kind. You know, the ones you feel like someone is going to grab your ankles as you walk, or run, up the steps!

When Patrick got home, and I told him about it but neither one of us had unplugged it. This was terrifying for me and when something like this happens, you tend to second guess yourself. Did that just really happen or was my mind playing tricks on me? You almost talk yourself out of it.

All I know is that it was loud and scared the daylight out of me. It was the only time this happened but every time I went downstairs to do laundry, I would go halfway down the steps and peek around the railing to see if the coast was clear.

Incidents like this went on so much that I would stop responding to the noises, however, the shadows always freaked me out. That was something I could never get used to.

As I was fast approaching my due date for my daughter, we had a combined birthday party for my son and my nephew at the Oakland house.

Now, I never spoke of the things going on in our house, because honestly, most people look at you like you have three heads. I could hear it now; Lynn's hormones are out of control with this pregnancy.

I mean, this was before computers were in every household and before reality TV would take over with every paranormal show you can think of.

Now there are so many paranormal and ghost shows on TV, everyone seems to be an expert, but back then, you really didn't hear about this stuff.

This was a time when Patrick thought he was cool sporting his bag cell phone. Oh Lord, looking back at it now, those things were hideous.

So, the party goes without a hitch, a good time had by all, but a few weeks later I was talking to my sister and she told me that our upstairs creeped her out. She was using the bathroom right across from Zian's room and she felt as if she was being watched. She told me she had goosebumps and the hair on the back of her neck was standing on end.

In a weird way, I was actually excited that someone other than the three of us, had experienced the same things upstairs.

It was validation.

This is where I finally told someone what was going on in the house. I was surprised she believed me but scared at the same time that she would be mad at me for having the family over now knowing what we had been through up until this point.

I'm glad nothing major happened, really nothing at all that we know of, because there were so many kids running in and out of the house. I don't think anyone would have noticed anyway, (unless someone's head did a 360 like Linda Blair's in The Exorcist), but for her to validate the same things I felt, meant the world to me.

It was the very reason I stopped taking showers in the upstairs bathroom. The eerie feeling of being watched, the goosebumps, your hair standing on end like there was an electric force field around your body, and finally, hearing your name being called when you are the only one in the house.

Now, even though Zian didn't always sleep in his room, almost all of his toys were up there. So, there were times he would go upstairs to grab a few toys and bring them downstairs so he could play, and sometimes he would just stay up there and play while I cleaned the house.

There were months when things would be quiet, and during one of these quiet months, we bought Zian a car bed to see if he wanted to sleep upstairs again since things seemed normal, or as normal as things can be.

As long as he felt comfortable, so were we.

He loved his little red Lamborghini bed (of course his daddy picked that one out) and started sleeping back in his room again, but ONLY if the lights were on, and we were good with that.

I'm not even sure how long it was, maybe a week or two and Zian would start coming back downstairs at, yep, 3:30 in the morning, only this time he would say, "There's a lady in my room!" Patrick and I both looked at each other confused, because up to this point, he always referred to it as a monster. Now he is telling us there is a lady up there?!

A few nights later, Patrick and I were sleeping when he woke up only to hear Zian screaming in his room. Patrick saw a dark black shadow figure, solid black, waving its arms to come towards it. He woke me up, jumped out of bed and ran upstairs to Zian. I had no clue what the hell was going on, all I knew was, I heard our son screaming upstairs and my husband was running like a bat out of hell to get to him.

Zian had a slight fever when he went to bed, so I thought maybe he was screaming because he didn't feel well. I couldn't have been more wrong.

When Patrick got upstairs, Zian was sitting in his car bed crying and telling him there is a monster in his room. Patrick was now leaning over Zian, and he was pointing over Patrick's shoulder, looking right through him like he wasn't even there. As he was looking over his shoulder like there was someone or something standing right behind him, Patrick felt a hand on his back and whipped around, but no one was there. At that time, the robot fan sitting on a tall speaker went flying across the room and the speaker flew in the opposite direction.

He grabbed Zian and ran down the steps and said to me, "He is no longer allowed to stay in that room!"

He looked absolutely terrified.

All I could see and hear from the bottom of the steps while all of this was going on was Zian crying, and then I heard the crash of the robot fan as it flew across the room and then saw the speaker topple over into the hallway, and that's when Patrick came running down the steps with our son.

I have never seen my husband so terrified in my life. He lost all of the color in his face, he was trembling and sweating profusely.

We stayed up the rest of the night and knew we had to do something.

The next morning, I would search for help in the Yellow Pages. I wasn't quite sure who or what I was looking for. Who do you call? What do you say? I certainly didn't want to say, "We need help, my three-year-old says there is a monster and a lady in his room!"

It's frustrating because you feel so alone.

So, while I'm flipping through the Yellow Pages looking for Psychics, I come across a Psychic Medium that is close to us.

What the hell do we have to lose, right?!

So, I called and informed them that we needed a cleansing in our house because there was some really weird stuff going on. I left it at that. I didn't tell them any details at ALL, and they didn't want to know either. To my surprise, they were eager to come out. The man I talked to said they would get in touch with us to come and investigate what was going on and bless our house.

Meanwhile, Zian would describe to us what the lady in his room looked like. He would say that she floats in his room and down the steps. He would tell us the best way a 3 yr. old knows how.

It wasn't until he was much older that he would give us more details on what he saw.

Pretty much at that time, all we knew was that there was a floating, legless lady in his room. He is 30 years old now and still remembers everything. He would tell us that her legs were missing but he could see her footsteps on the carpet. There was one time he told us when he was laying in his bed, he would see footprint impressions in the carpet when she came around the corner from the hallway, and she would then sit at the end of his bed and stare at him, but he could only see the top half of her. She wouldn't say anything, she would just stare at him.

He would also tell us about the monster in his room. He described it as just a head with big red eyes that would come out of the ceiling fan in his room. This ceiling fan didn't have a light, it was strictly a fan.

After hearing this, you think, what kind of horrible parents were we to make him sleep in his room all this time he was telling us there was a monster in his room. But that's what kids do right?! Make up stories and see imaginary friends and monsters?!

Before this incident took place, Patrick tells me that his friend from high school needs a place to stay with her 2-year-old, because her husband who is in the military is being stationed overseas. They lived in Georgia at the time and she didn't want to move overseas with the baby. So, she was going to move back up North and just needed a place to stay until she could land a job and find an apartment. We didn't hesitate to have them come stay with us. Besides, it will be good for Zian to have a friend to play with, even if just for a little while.

When Pam and her baby girl, Megan, arrived at our house, we set them up in our son's room.

I know, I know, that sounds horrible, but honestly, since Zian was sleeping downstairs most of the time until the last encounter, we really just didn't even think about it.

I guess a part of us hoped they would see something just to validate we weren't CRAZY!

We had already told her they could stay with us before that terrifying evening, and things never seemed to happen when we had company over anyway.

We have had many people over to our house and not one person ever experienced anything, other than my sister saying our upstairs bathroom creeped her out. Maybe this would give us a break.

Things were quiet for the most part after that night, other than the mail that was coming to our house, addressed to Virginia. I would put in the china cabinet, and on occasion, it would be found opened or moved the next day. Now, that was my own little secret that I didn't even tell my husband about at first. When I would receive Virginia's mail, I would say, "Virginia, if you're the one in my house, I have your mail and I'm going to put it in your China cabinet for you! Feel free to open it!" I knew the house was newly purchased by my landlord, so I could only assume that the mail coming to our house was for the previous owner, because she told us the owner of the house passed and that's how it came up for sale. There were days that I would put the mail in the cabinet and a couple of hours later I would find one of the doors open and the mail moved, and sometimes opened. I couldn't blame Patrick for this because he was at work, and besides, he had no clue I was doing this, and the man NEVER touched the china cabinet, and our son was too small to even reach the door, much less the mail at the very top where I placed it. We would even find old jewelry in the house, it looked like something my grandmother would wear, but we didn't know where it was coming from. It would just show up.

After about a week of staying with us, Megan was sick with a fever. The next morning when Pam woke up, she looked at me and said, "Thank you for checking on Megan in the middle of the night! That was so sweet of you!" I looked at her and then my husband, (I'm sure with the most confused look on my face) and said, "I wasn't up there, that wasn't me! Did you go up there last night Patrick?!" He was shaking his head no with wide eyes. Pam then said, "No, it was a woman! Come on, Lynn, I know it was you!" chuckling.

I'm sure she thought we were pulling her leg, but I was dumbfounded.

"No, Pam! I haven't been upstairs in months, unless I have to grab Zian's clothes or toys, but other than that, nope, I don't go up there!" I said.

Now I can see the look of concern on her face as it went from smiling to a face of shock. She then says, "Then who was the lady that came into our room last night, sat on the edge of the bed and put her hand on Megan's head?! She looked like she was feeling for a temperature! I thought it was you, so I went back to sleep!"

Patrick and I then told her what had been going on in the house but that things had been quiet, so we really didn't think much about it.

I thought about reaching over and lightly pushing her jaw back up from hitting the ground during our moment of awkward silence. I could tell this information was too much for her to handle at the time.

After Pam soaked in this information, she had to leave for a job interview, which I'm sure she was praying all the way there that she got the job so she could move out. I know I would have been if I was in her shoes.

People have asked us all of the time, why didn't you just move? It wasn't that simple. I wish it were, but it just wasn't. Both of us were very young when we got married, we weren't established yet and we were just barely making ends meet that early in our lives. We put everything we had into renting that house to make a home for our family. Our intentions were to someday buy it and make it our own. We didn't have the money to just pick up and leave, as much as we wanted to.

So, now Pam has left for her job interview and Patrick was leaving for work which left me alone with the kiddos for the day.

Oh boy, I had no clue what the day would bring.

Zian loved to play with his action figures in the kitchen sink, which kept him out of my hair for a bit to get things done around the house or just rest on the couch for a moment to put my big swollen feet up like the Dr. told me too.

While Zian and Megan were playing on the living room floor and I was watching TV, he asked to play in the sink.

We had a pretty good routine, he would put his toys, mostly Batman action figures (as this child was obsessed with Batman), in the left side of the double sink and I would fill the right side up with water. He would then scoot the kitchen chair over and hop up and play for hours at times. He had already thrown all of his toys in the sink when he grabbed me by the hand and helped me off the couch.

He was always such a good helper while I was pregnant.

So now he was holding my right hand and Megan was holding my left hand and as we rounded the corner from the living room to the kitchen, I saw the water turn on and the faucet moved from the left side of the sink to the right side. I FROZE! Right there in my tracks, when Zian said

"SEE! There she is mommy!"

I could not see her, but I DID SEE the movement of the knobs and the faucet. I DID SEE the water coming out!

I grabbed each child under each arm like footballs and ran right out the front door.

As I sat on the front porch just trembling, I noticed Zian seemed quite calm and was not scared in the least after what we just saw.

Maybe there was a monster and a lady?! After all, his reaction was always calm when he would tell us there was a lady in his room, but he would be terrified when he talked about the monster.

As a matter of fact, he seemed happy that I saw what he did and continued playing on the porch as if nothing happened.

Outside was a beautiful sunny day and on the inside was darkness. I didn't know what to do. I looked around outside, and it was absolutely beautiful.

People doing yard work, playing with their kids, walking their dogs, and here I was, terrified out of my mind of what was in my house.

After I collected myself, (because I'm trying to keep it together for the kids) I went back inside fearing the water was running all over the kitchen floor.

When we went back in, I had the kids stay by the front door in the living room while I peeked my head around the corner to see what kind of mess was in there. To my amazement, the water was off, and the sink was half full just like I used to fill it for him.

We got through the rest of the day by sitting mostly on the front porch, thank goodness it was a big porch and both of the kids loved to play outside. While the kids were playing on the porch, the incident would play over and over again in my head like a bad record. The more I thought about it, the more I realized, whatever it was, wasn't trying to hurt us.

At least not like the encounter we had in Zian's room.

Did we have more than one ghost or entity in our house?

Like I said previously, this isn't something you really heard about back then. By this time in my life, I saw Amityville Horror and The Exorcist, but this was all we had to go by, so that was terrifying to think about.

Was my child going to start spewing pea soup across the room and my walls begin to bleed?!

So naturally, I wasn't too surprised when I told Pam and Patrick what had happened, that Pam immediately started packing their belongings.

They were gone that night and went to stay with another family member. I can't say that I didn't blame her, we would have left too if we could have.

## Chapter Five

## The House Blessing

Today was the day our house was going to be blessed. We were excited yet terrified of the unknown. Would they be able to clear our house? Would they be able to help us at all? I have to tell you; both of our heads were spinning.

I couldn't believe they were finally here, and we were going to get some help. (I'm sorry, after 27 years I can't remember their names, so I'll call them Jenny and Joe for the telling of the events). We were eagerly awaiting them on our porch. They both appeared to be in their early 40's and just average people. I think Joe may have been a Minister, as he had his bible and Holy water in hand. Jenny was definitely the Medium, she was slowly walking up to the house looking around and you could tell she was just soaking things in. I remember her stopping on the sidewalk and she looked at the window on the 2nd story and she was just staring, for what seemed like forever. Her eyes were fixed on Zian's room. I could tell she was already getting vibes from the house, it looked as though it was speaking to her and she was just listening. I have to tell you, I just wanted to crawl inside her head and see what she was seeing or feeling. I still didn't know how a Medium worked, what they did, what they saw, or anything.

I'm not going to lie, all I pictured in my head was Zelda Rubinstein, the short Medium in Poltergeist! I was happy when I saw Jenny get out of that car instead. I don't know if I could have handled a little Zelda and our son's toys flying around in his room like a tornado. I don't think we could have handled that, but I think that was what was going through both of our heads.

Joe made his way up to us with a smile on his face with an extended hand to my husband. He introduced himself and then turned to introduce Jenny as she was slowly making her way up to us. Once she got on the steps, and we all shook hands and introduced ourselves, I saw the smile on Jenny's face go away and turn to concern as her eyes saw my big pregnant belly. She immediately said, "You can't be in there when we do this. You have a clean soul in you, and I can't take the chance with that!" All the while, what was going through my head was, ohhhhh no you don't, you are not going to deny me this! Jenny then said, "You can do the walk through with us but when it comes to connecting to the Spirit you will have to step out with your son!" I was good with that actually. I didn't want Zian in there when that was going on, because all I was picturing in my head was the priests in the Exorcist and Amityville Horror getting violently ill while things were flying around the house. She asked us not to say anything as she was reading the house during her walk through. Jenny told us we can walk behind her, and she would tell us what she was picking up on, but not to validate anything until she was finished. Joe didn't say much, you could tell Jenny was in charge.

Jenny walked in the front door and into our living room. She stood in the doorway and looked around. She was quiet, not saying anything. She slowly started towards the dining room and then went directly into the kitchen with us all in tow. She stopped abruptly. I thought we were all going to pile into one another like a bad wreck on the highway in the middle of a blizzard the way we were walking so close to one another, trying not to miss anything she said. She looked to her right, which was the door to the hallway that led up to Zian's room. We had been keeping it shut because it just made us feel a little more at ease. It's not like you can shut a door and the ghost is now stuck on the other side of it, but it was something, and it certainly made Zian feel better.

So, now she was opening the door and took a step up to the landing. She stopped, took a few deep breaths and grabbed her chest. Jenny then said, "She died right here." Patrick and I just looked at each other and our eyes were wide, trying not to make a sound. Jenny started up the steps and she had her hands on the walls as she walked. Her head slightly tilted back and her hands gently touching the wallpaper as she slowly took each step. When she got to the top, she stopped and said, "The wallpaper is yellow underneath!" Once again Patrick and I looked at one another and shrugging our shoulders because we didn't know what any of this meant. Now

she was on the landing at the top of the steps, she was standing in front of a closet, she looked right into the bathroom and then to the left into Zian's room. Drawn to the bedroom, she walked in. We were all cramped on the steps now trying to get into the room, so we didn't miss anything she had to say. She almost looked like she was in a trance while walking through the house and telling us what she saw. Jenny then said, "It happened in there!" pointing to the bathroom. Jenny told us the lady of the house was in her sewing closet when she started to get chest pains so she tried making her way into her sewing room, which was Zian's room, not fully understanding what was happening to her, she then tried to make it down the stairs to call for help but ended up falling down them. She would die on the landing. At least, this is what Jenny told us. As we were standing in Zian's bedroom, dumbfounded by what she just told us, she asked me if the bathroom used to be a walk-in closet. I told Jenny it has always been a bathroom since we lived there but I could always ask the owner. She then told us about the lady who died on the bottom landing, her name started with a V and she lived here for a long time. (Well that explained the mail we were getting for a Virginia). She also told us that she wasn't found immediately and may have laid on the steps for a week or two before being found.
We would later find out that her children lived out of state and her husband was deceased.

    Jenny headed back downstairs so she could walk around the rest of the house. She then told me I had to leave the house with Zian at this point, so she and Joe could cleanse the house. This was the part where Joe came in. He had been pretty quiet up to this point, but he would be leading the prayer throughout the house and spreading the Holy water.

    Zian and I went outside on the porch and Patrick stayed inside with Joe and Jenny for what seemed like forever. They finally came outside and asked that we bring Zian in, to see if he would go upstairs and see if he can feel anything.

    Patrick is visibly upset; I could tell he had been crying. I wanted to know what happened in there, but I would find out soon enough.

As soon as we stepped in the house, I could just tell things felt different. It felt good. Jenny asked Zian to go up to his room and without hesitation, he went up the steps and into his room. He ran up those steps like I had not seen him do in a very long time. He got to the top of the steps, went into his room, and peeped his head around the corner to the hall steps as we were making our way up and said, "Yup! She's gone!" We were so relieved. Jenny asked him if he wanted to stay in his room again and Zian answered back with an enthusiastic "YES!"

We had our house back.

Joe handed us the Holy water and told us to keep it. He let us know we could sprinkle the Holy water in the house anytime we wanted to, and that Patrick knew what to do since he was in there with them when they blessed the house.

By the way, I STILL have that same bottle of Holy water to this day.

We gave our hugs and said our goodbyes and off they went.

Patrick told me what happened when we stepped outside. Joe, Jenny, and Patrick sat in the living room. Jenny was telling Virginia to go to the light and that she had passed on. Virginia told Jenny she won't go into the light because Patrick has an attachment. Virginia would tell Jenny that a spirit named Jeff has been with Patrick for a while and was attached to him. Patrick burst into tears.

Jeff was his best friend that was killed in a car crash in high school. This was something that even I didn't know.

Virginia also stated to Jenny that she wasn't trying to scare us and that she was just trying to help around the house and with the kids while I was pregnant.

This all made sense now. The faucet that turned on, the lady that checked on Megan when she had a fever, and the dryer running when I went to do laundry. But what about the figure in the doorway and the episode in Zian's room when the robot fan and speaker were thrown? Those weren't friendly at all.

Jenny said there was also a dark presence in the house as well but felt confident that she could send it on its way. She also mentioned that Jeff was with Patrick when he had his motorcycle accident shortly after moving into the house. (Another thing that wasn't disclosed to them). Even the police officer that was behind Patrick when a car turned in front of him while riding his motorcycle thought for sure he was going to be looking at a dead man lying in the middle of the street. He didn't have his helmet on, T-boned a car that turned in his path and landed on his head. By all means, he should have died that day, but now we know Jeff was with him during that crash. He spent a few days in the hospital but other than a broken neck that would require a neck brace and a black eye with a few stitches, he was in relatively good shape.

We also put two and two together about the shadow figure Patrick saw in our previous apartment when I had my migraine when Zian was just six months old. You remember, the one that walked from the bathroom to the bedroom when I was lying down? This had to be Jeff.

Is this also who Zian was seeing in the apartment when he was having his night terrors or the voice we were hearing on the monitor?

So, after they got Virginia and Jeff to go into the light, and Patrick told Jeff it's okay to go, Joe and Jenny cleansed the house of the dark entity through prayer and using the Holy water.

Now we had a gazillion questions, but at least we had our home back. Our house seemed so light and full of happiness again.

Zian was sleeping through the nights in his own room and we were finally getting some sleep.

## Chapter Six

## Digging for Answers

Now that we had our house and sanity back, I decided to do a little digging into the Oakland house. I figured my best bet would be to start with my landlord, but before I did that, I decided to pull up some of the wallpaper in the upstairs hallway. I needed to know if the wallpaper was yellow underneath, like Jenny said it was.

So, I tried to find a corner of the wallpaper that I could pull up without doing any major damage, I just wanted a tiny peek. I finally found a spot in the middle of the hall where the seams meet. I pulled it ever so slowly, trying not to rip the paper, but I was scared to death to look. I was sweating bullets because I had a big enough section pulled up and now, I needed to see if Jenny was right. I slowly peeked under the paper and when I saw the YELLOW wall underneath, I jumped. I was breathing heavily, almost to the point of hyperventilating, and I jumped back and hit my back on the other side of the hallway wall. Jenny was right!

After getting up the nerve to call my landlord, Mandy, and after many rehearsals of what I was going to say, I finally picked up the phone and called. I still wasn't quite sure how this was going to go because I had to tell her that we had a Medium come over to our house and cleanse it.

When I called, Mandy answered the phone, and I asked if I could ask her a few questions about the house. So, I jumped right in there and asked if the upstairs bathroom used to be a walk-in closet. Mandy seemed confused and said,

"Yes, how did you know that? We had the upstairs remodeled and that used to be the previous owners sewing closet. It's where she kept all of her sewing stuff?"

Without answering her question, I then asked her if the previous owner died in the house, specifically at the bottom of the hallway landing, and if she lay there for a couple of weeks before she was discovered. Her reply would blow me away! Mandy said,

"Oh my God! Is the smell coming through? Does the house stink? I'm sorry we thought we got rid of the smell."

"No, Mandy, the house doesn't stink, but IT IS true? She died on the landing of the hallway? Was her name Virginia? Was that Virginia's china cabinet?" I said to her. I didn't let her get in a word as I was rambling off question after question.

Mandy said that when they bought the house, the upstairs was a sewing room and a walk-in closet, so they decided to turn the closet into a bathroom. She told me that the previous owner DID die on the landing and that she had been there for a while before she was found.

Apparently, Virginia lived alone after her husband passed away and her children lived in different states. So, when her children didn't hear from her, they had the police do a welfare check. That was when Virginia was found.

She asked me what was going on, so I told her Zian has been seeing a lady in his room and I went into detail about the things going on in the house. When I finished, I heard laughter on the other end with her saying.

"I have had people come up with some pretty good excuses to get out of rent, but this takes the cake, Lynn."

I was not amused after everything we had gone through and not to mention I was weeks away from delivering our second child and my hormones were raging. I answered her with a very stern;

"I am NOT kidding Mandy! How do you think I know all of this, Mandy?"

That question got her attention. It made her think, because back then, I couldn't GOOGLE my address, and even if I could, I wouldn't know about the details of the inside of the house.

She then told me that when they bought the house it needed a lot of updating, not to mention getting rid of the stench from a rotting corpse. So, while they were renovating the house, her two sons stayed there while the work was going on and while they attended college.

They only stayed there a year though, before renting it out, and we were her first tenants in that house.

Mandy said she was going to call her sons and ask them if they ever noticed anything. I wasn't holding my breath for a call back, but low and behold, Mandy called me back a few hours later.

When I answered the phone, she said, "Lynn, you were right. One of my son's said he couldn't sleep upstairs because the lights would turn off and on while he was sleeping, he would hear footsteps around his bed and knocks in the hallway. So, he started sleeping on the couch in the living room, and my other son said he would see shadows while he was lying in bed and also hear footsteps." You could hear the excitement in her voice as she was telling me this.

I was shocked she even called me back, but I was even more shocked when she told me her sons were experiencing the same things we were. To be honest, I was dancing a little victory dance in my living room while she was telling me this.

She was surprised they didn't tell her, but then again, look at how she reacted to me. I'm not surprised at all. It's not an easy thing to tell people. Well, now it is, because it's widely accepted. Back then, NO WAY. Nowadays people pay good money to go to haunted houses and do haunted tours, I just lived it with my family.

Well now that I had some answers to my questions, I could turn my attention to my baby girl who would be making her appearance a couple of weeks earlier than expected.

## Chapter Seven

## Not Again

Things were great since the cleansing of the house. I gave birth to our daughter Teall, and Zian had been overjoyed by his new baby sister, but of course he had been making it very clear what toys she could and couldn't play with. He was a great helper when it came to his little sister, he was a natural protector.

I remember the first night Teall came home and I had to get up every two hours to check on her, not because she was crying, but because she was sleeping. She never woke up. Her first night she slept eight hours, straight through the night. Surely, she had to be hungry or have a wet diaper. It was never ending, me standing over her with my hand on her back just making sure she was breathing. After a couple of days of this, I called the doctor because I thought something was wrong with her. He assured me it was normal and if she were hungry, she would let me know.

To this day, that girl can sleep. One day when she was a teenager, she told Patrick she was going to take a nap, she woke up the next day. Fifteen hours later. It wasn't until she was three years old that we would find out she was anemic and that played a very big role in her sleeping patterns.

Nevertheless, it was a big change from what we were used to with Zian. It was always in the back of my mind though, you know, would Teall end up like Zian someday? Would she have night terrors? Would she be able to see things we can't? Would she have the gift her older brother has? I had so many questions, but I just kept them tucked away in the back of my mind, crossing my fingers just hoping we wouldn't have a repeat of her big brother. I figured there was no sense in worrying about it now, she was just an infant.

After my maternity leave was over, it was time to get back to work. Working in a restaurant with an infant and a toddler was very challenging, to say the least. Being in a management position I worked a lot of crazy hours and Patrick worked in landscaping, so his hours were also long and tedious. I honestly don't know how we managed back then. Thank God for good family and friends because there weren't many people we trusted our kids with.

Depending on my schedule we didn't always need a sitter for the kids. If I worked the night shift, Patrick was home with the kids and if I worked the afternoon shift, we only needed a sitter for a couple of hours until he got home. It was the dreaded morning shift when I had to open the restaurant. I had to get up at 4 a.m. and then Patrick had to be at work at 7 or 8 in the morning.

I know you all get it. We all understand the struggles of a two-income family, it's no different now than it was back then. Juggling a family and careers can be quite challenging.

We had a great little street, lots of kids and lots of great families. Zian had kids his own age that lived on both sides of us, so he was always outside playing with the other kids while us parents would sit outside and watch them play. I'm just grateful my kids got to experience a childhood before electronics and cell phones would take over in just a few years.

Through one of the neighbors, we met a 19-year-old girl named Louis. We weren't that much older than her, seeing we were in our early twenties. She loved our kids and Zian really took to her. She became a fixture in our household. Louis didn't have the best family structure, so I think she was seeking solace in our little family. She was a breath of fresh air, to be honest. She had a great sense of humor and was just fun to be around. If Patrick were at work, Louis would watch the kids so I could get some rest. We loved having her around.

When Louis didn't want to stay at home because things were bad, we would let her spend the night at our place. This way we knew she was safe and not out on the streets getting into trouble when her parents would decide to kick her out, during one of their drunken rages. This became our new normal. Since Louis was nineteen and out of school, we told her she could stay with us and she could watch the kids when Patrick and I were working. It was a win-win. She didn't have to pay for rent or food and in exchange, she would watch the kids for us and have a safe place to stay.

A few months in, I started noticing things being misplaced in the house. You know, like your car keys being moved or your favorite shirt suddenly goes missing and then a week or two later, that same shirt suddenly pops up in the place you looked for it the first time. Just little things that would make you scratch your head and leave you wondering if you just missed it the first time you looked. Then you brush it off and go about your business. Now it was starting to happen to my husband, things of his would go missing or they were in a spot he didn't leave them. We would get into arguments about this because he thought Zian, Lois, or myself were moving his things.

The mood in the house seemed to shift. It just felt different. It almost had that uneasy dark feeling like I used to feel when the hauntings started the first time. The hair on the back of my neck would start to stand like there was an electric current in the air and I always felt like I was being watched. I definitely didn't like being alone, but I also didn't tell anyone how I was feeling. I certainly didn't want to freak out Zian or Patrick, and of course we had discussed it with Louis when we met her, it's not like we kept it a secret or anything. Heck, she even slept in the basement by her choice, it didn't bother her a bit.

So, one evening we were coming home from a night out with the kids (Louis had left earlier), when I heard our neighbor yell with a southern twang (they were from the south and had a very distinct country or hillbilly accent as my husband would like to say)

"Hey Lynn, we were just sittin' on the porch and couldn't help but notice your lights kept going off and on in y'alls house while y'all were gone. It looked like a disco in there. Looks like y'alls ghosts are back!"

*This just can't be happening.* Sure enough, every single light was on in the house. Being a family that lived from paycheck to paycheck, we were on a very strict budget. We would turn off every light in the house and just leave on the porch light along with the lamp in the living room when we were gone.

One good thing about having a neighbor like Nellie is that nothing gets by her without her noticing. Hell, I remember one day we decided to rearrange the house and we moved the fish tank to the other side of the living room. The kids were in bed and Patrick and I were snuggled on the couch watching some T.V. when we heard a loud obnoxious voice (trust me, when Nellie spoke, you knew it was her)

"Hey guys, I love y'alls fish tank there better! Looks real nice and all wit da lights all out and stuff. It shines mighty nice! Very purty!"

Nellie was definitely our eyes and ears when we weren't home, and unfortunately, when we were home.

This was the point where Patrick and I started sharing some feelings and concerns we were having about the house. He was also feeling like the house had shifted, it felt darker to him too. We both had our guards up, that was for sure.

It wouldn't take long after this incident for Zian to start waking up in the middle of the night and climbing into our bed again. He would tell us there was a monster in his room again and it was keeping him awake at night. Zian told us that he saw a red glow come from his ceiling fan and it yelled "LEAVE" and then his room shook. His toys would fly off of his dresser and turn on by themselves. This absolutely terrified me, it terrified us both. I don't understand, the house was cleansed, and things were going so well. What happened? What changed? *Why is this happening again?*

One night we were watching T.V. and we heard a loud bang in the kitchen, just like before when we heard the sound of pots and pans hitting the floor, only this time when we went to investigate, every cabinet door was open and pots and pans were actually laying on the floor. The footsteps and the shadows started again. I remember Patrick yelling, looking up towards Zian's room telling whatever it was to STOP. He would say, "This is our house now." We were both assuming maybe Virginia didn't go into the light and now she was angry.

When I would go to work, I would tell my friends what was going on. I would vent to my friends and they would always say they wanted to check it out for themselves. I had two friends that weren't believers, so I challenged them to spend ONE night in Zian's room.

Now in hindsight, that may not have been a good idea, but they jumped on the offer. Sometimes you just want to prove to yourself that you're not crazy and hope others can experience what we have. An "I told you so" moment, I guess.

It's just tiring thinking you are walking alone with the paranormal. I know I'm not alone in the sense that my husband and son have been through this terrifying experience together, but alone in the sense of no one believes you when you tell them, or they think you're crazy and laugh at you.

We decided on a night and Trevor and Missy came with their pillows and sleeping bags in hand. They looked like they were on a camping trip. They even had a bunch of snacks to munch on for their little slumber party. We had them go straight upstairs and wished them good luck.

Patrick and I were watching T.V. for about an hour while they were upstairs. We could hear them up there laughing and having a great time. It was kind of frustrating because nothing was happening. So, Louis and Patrick decided they would knock on the ceiling to scare them. They were giggling like a couple of schoolgirls when Patrick took the end of a broom handle and started hitting the ceiling. The next thing we heard was, "Nice try you guys, we know that was you!"

Defeated, we all decided to call it a night and went to bed. A few hours later at 3:30 a.m. sharp, we heard both Trevor and Missy screaming at the top of their lungs. It sounded like there was a WWF fight going on up there. The next thing we know, they are running down the steps with all of their stuff in their arms, dropping belongings as they were running out the front door. We were trying to stop them to see what the hell happened, but they weren't sticking around for commentary. They jumped in the car and took off.

Patrick, Louis, and I went upstairs but I was the first idiot to go up the steps. As I got to the top of the steps, I felt two hands on my behind and then I was shoved up the steps and fell into the closet at the top of the hallway. I turned to look at Patrick to curse him out because I thought he was playing a prank on me, but to my surprise, both Patrick and Louis were at the bottom of the steps, with the look of sheer terror in their eyes. He said, "What the hell just happened?" and I replied, "I was just shoved up the steps into the closet! That wasn't YOU??"

As he was answering me with a "NO" I looked into Zian's room and it looked like a freight train went through it. By this time, all three of us were in the bedroom just looking at the mayhem. Everything was strewn about the room. Toys, clothes, lamps, you name it. What did we just do? What did we unleash in our house? Now I saw the movie Poltergeist and his room looked like it came right out of the scene from that movie.

The next morning, I talked to Trevor and asked him what the hell happened up there. He told me at first, they both heard footsteps walking around them. He thought maybe it was us sneaking up the steps, but when they both looked, they could see the depressions in the carpet as they heard the walking. They were both frozen in fear when the lights started to flicker off and on and then things were starting to fall off shelves, toys were turning on and moving and that was when they both bailed. He told me he was sorry he ever doubted me.

That was it. I picked up the phone and called Jenny. Louis and I were sitting in my living room when I made the call. When Jenny answered the phone, I just blurted out,

"IT'S HAPPENING AGAIN JENNY AND NOW IT'S PISSED!"

She told me to calm down because by this point, I was in tears. I told her everything was great for a while and then things just went to shit. It wasn't like the last time. This was mean and evil. It physically moves things and it pushed me into a closet. I was yelling at poor Jenny, telling her she must have pissed off Virginia for trying to get her to leave what used to be her house.

Jenny then asked me if there was a young female sitting next to me. When I told her yes, she asked me to leave the room where I could talk freely and away from her. I was really perplexed by this because I didn't even tell her Louis was there. As a matter of fact, Jenny didn't even know we had anyone staying with us.

Once I excused myself from Louis, I told Jenny I was alone. The very next thing that came out of Jenny's mouth was,

"Lynn! You HAVE to get rid of her!!"

I was floored. "What the hell are you talking about, Jenny?' I said to her.

She told me that this wasn't Virginia we were dealing with. She said Virginia and Jeff went to the light and that Louis brought this with her to our house. I was so confused; my head was spinning. Jenny explained to me that some people can have attachments and they will follow them wherever they go. In our case, Louis had a poltergeist attached to her and if we were not careful, we could get stuck with it. I had to pinch myself because I couldn't believe what I was hearing. This just couldn't be. Jenny said once she leaves our house for good, she would come back and do another cleansing, but not until Louis was GONE.

Once I got off the phone with Jenny, I needed some time to gather my thoughts. I finally confronted Louis. First off, what do you say? Excuse me but do you attract ghosts? In reality, there really is no good way to ask someone or in our case, blame someone for bringing a nasty ghost to their house.

So, I just came out with it and asked Louis if she had any attachments that she knew of. To my surprise, she answered with a yes. She told me she had a ghost at her house too. She said she thought it sometimes followed her, but she wasn't sure. As she was telling me this, she had this smirk on her face like it was funny. I was livid. This little talk we were having turned into a full-blown yelling match. I was furious that she knew all along that she had an attachment and knew what we had just gone through and she STILL didn't say anything.

When Patrick got home and I filled him in, it was over. We sent her packing. We were not taking any chances with our family.

Immediately we called Jenny and Joe and had them come cleanse the house.

Once again, we had our house back. Well, at least we hoped we did. Our track record at this point wasn't looking too good.

We would live in the Oakland house for another 4 years without any incidents other than Zian and Teall seeing our black cat, Bear, in the basement after he died. This was something I didn't learn about until they were both teenagers. By this time Zian was eight and Teall was five years old when we moved from the Oakland house and he knew he was different from other kids his age, therefore there were things he didn't tell me about so he wouldn't freak out his dad and me.

## Chapter Eight

## Acceptance

After six years in the Oakland house, it was time to move on. My mother-in-law wanted to buy a two-family house so we could all live together. Although this wasn't in our long-term goals and not in the area we necessarily wanted to live, we decided to do it for a short term, until we found the house we wanted, in the school district we wanted our kids to go to school in.

We were all excited about the move, especially the kids, but I have to say, I was worried what this house would bring. It was an old three-story house that was built in 1907. The woodwork was magnificent, this turn of the century home had the original hardwoods, railings, woodwork throughout the house. You could tell it had a lot of history and could probably tell stories, and that worried me.

I remember walking through the house with the kids and watching them both, especially Zian, because I wanted to see if they picked up on anything. You could just see the history in this house, and you knew it was very old because of the architecture and it needed a lot of work. There were cracks all over the walls and the heating system was the original to the house, you know, the old steam heaters that would scorch you if you touched it. The floors were slanted from the years and years of the house settling. When you walked in the kitchen it felt like you were walking down a slight hill, but this house was perfect until we bought our own house.

Every time I heard a creak or a thump in the house my heart would drop, and I would freeze in my tracks. This old house made so many noises, the hardwood floors would sound like someone was walking on them in the middle of the night when the house was settling. It took a few months to get to know what all of the sounds were, like the pipes banging when the heater kicked on or the loud noises you would hear when you turned on the water or flushed a toilet. Every typical sound that you would expect to hear in a haunted house, well, we had them there.

While living there, I started my journey to become a police officer. I had worked at my job for fifteen years at this point, but I wasn't happy at all. I wanted to follow my dream. My husband was very supportive, but it was very scary, to say the least, because if I made it, I didn't even know if I was cut out for the job. This was my childhood dream, but I would be tested like I've never been tested before. It seemed like I would get so far in the process and then I would get eliminated. It was frustrating but I wasn't going to give up. It just made me train harder.

During this time, we got a devastating phone call in the middle of the night. My husband's cousin, Lewis, was killed in a car accident. This was a crushing blow to Patrick; they were as close as brothers. Lewis was at our house at least 3 times a week. He had two very young children and a wonderful wife. Our hearts were broken for them. This was our first significant loss we had since we had been married and it was tough to explain to the kids. He was so young, in his early thirties.

Little did I know his death would touch me in ways I never knew possible. Shortly after he died, I was disqualified from the recruiting process, AGAIN. This was the fourth and final time. I was done with trying. After I got the dreaded letter of disqualification and after crying all day because my dreams were shattered, I went to bed dejected.

That evening I had a dream, and Lewis and my aunt Joanie were in it. They both told me that the disqualification was a mistake and that I needed to fight it. They told me not to give up.

When I woke up, I didn't know what to think. The dream was so real. I felt like they were both still in the room with me when I woke up. I could feel their presence. I remember going down into the basement, or the dungeon as the kids would say, and told Patrick I was going to fight this. I wasn't quitting. I could see the confusion on his face because just the day before I was telling him how I was done trying to be a police officer. I was so dejected but now I had a new light shining over me.

So, from there, I called to set up a civil service hearing so I could dispute the disqualification. They gave me a date to show up and you better bet I was there. I was fired up and determined to speak my mind. Little did I know when I got there, there would be a room full of thirty or more people waiting to dispute their rejection letters too. I have to say I was a little deflated by the time they got through half of the room, listening to everyone's excuses on why they should be reinstated into the process. Even the board members that were made up of a couple of officers and the rest civilians that worked for the city, you could tell they lost interest. So, wouldn't you know, I was the very last person sitting in the room and it was finally my turn. I was pretty aggravated at this point because I felt that what I was about to say was going to fall on deaf ears. I told them that I was just as aggravated as they were having to listen to the multiple reasons why people thought they should be reinstated into the police recruit process. I just said what I had to say, and I got up and left the room. I didn't give them a chance to say anything to me, I just walked out of the room. I knew I just blew any chance I had, but low and behold a few days later I got my reinstatement letter in the mail. I WAS BACK IN THE RECRUIT PROCESS. I couldn't believe it. Lewis and aunt Joanie really did send me a message through a dream. They were right.

 This would be the first dream I had since I was a child that felt like a message. Some of my messages I would understand clearly, and others would take years or a lifetime to finally understand.

 After spending three years in this beautiful house, without any paranormal experiences, the time had finally come to buy our own home, Zian now eleven, and Teall eight years old. We moved into a little red brick cape cod with three bedrooms and a huge front and backyard. It was right across the street from the grade school and church I went to as a kid and reminded me of the house I grew up in, that was just a couple of blocks away, where my mom and dad still lived.

 Once again, we would be watching the kids like a hawk when we did our walk through of the house. Although it had been almost seven years since we had any experiences it was still fresh in our minds. We also didn't know if Teall could sense the things her brother could. Up until this point, she had never said anything and we didn't ask any questions.

The kids were excited to pick the two bedrooms upstairs and we would take the downstairs bedroom, the smallest bedroom in the house of course. Boy, the things we give up for our children. Teall was happy with her smaller bedroom upstairs because it had a door for privacy and Zian of course was ecstatic because he got the master bedroom, which was huge for an eleven-year-old. Both of their rooms had dressers and bookshelves made of hardwood built into the walls. They were gorgeous.

I wouldn't notice anything out of the ordinary when we first moved in, except the fact that Zian and I became more in tune with one another. What I mean by that is, I could be sitting on the couch, thinking about how I needed him to take out the garbage, and before you know it, I would hear him running down the steps and he would say, "Did you call me, Mom?" It would freak me out. I would respond, "No, but I was about to call you down to take out the garbage though!" He would just say "OK" and head out the door with the garbage in hand like it was no big deal. This happened more times than I could count, and it worked both ways, as Zian started to notice the same thing.

At this point, I was still trying to get into the Police Academy, so when I would get home from work, I would run three to four miles every day. I was almost in my mid-thirties so running wasn't something I was used to after having two children. I was active as a kid and I played soccer for almost fifteen years, but man was I out of shape.

Patrick was a gem because he left landscaping for a bit and worked part time while the kids were in school so he could shuttle them back and forth to school and whatever other activities they had going on. Working as a salary manager I worked a lot of nights and weekends and a lot of times I was working up to sixty hours a week. I couldn't thank Patrick enough for giving up a job he loved doing just so I could follow my dreams. I knew he was a keeper the first day I laid eyes on him.

The street we lived on was a main drag, a four-lane road with lots and lots of traffic. On both sides of us, our neighbors were older and both had lived in their houses for fifty plus years, but two doors up from us was a family close to our age and they had a son that still lived at home that was Zian's age. Zian and Teall played with Paul all of the time. Either they were at our house or they were at his.

Zian would start to see shadow figures out in the backyard when they were playing, he said it would peep over the fence like it was watching them, but I didn't find this out until he was thirty years old. He told me he didn't want to freak us out, so he kept it to himself. To this day it saddens me that he felt he needed to keep this from us, but I get it. Patrick and I were very frightened and nervous in the past when we saw shadows but Zian were more accepting of his gift. Even though it scared him too, he felt the need to protect his parents and sister. I always said he was an old soul.

The next significant thing that I would remember after moving there was 9/11, the terror attacks on the Twin Towers in NYC.

9-11-2001: This is a day we will all remember, right?! I mean, most of us can recall exactly what we were doing when the first plane hit the Towers. I was in the middle of a dream when Patrick came and woke me up to tell me that a plane hit the twin towers. I had worked late the night before and Patrick had already dropped the kids off at school. So, when he woke me up, I was confused because the dream was so real, and I was trying to grasp what he was now telling me. My dream was that my aunt Joanie, who had passed in the '80s, was pulling me in for a hug and as we were embracing, I suddenly found myself standing to the side watching. My aunt Joanie was still hugging someone, but it wasn't me. Then when they stepped back from one another, it was my aunt Joanie and my aunt Vicky. This was the moment my husband woke me up.

To clear up my family dynamics, my mom is the oldest of three siblings. My aunt Vicky and aunt Joanie were my two favorite aunts' because they were both absolutely hilarious. Aunt

Joanie was the youngest of the sisters and she died from breast cancer in the 1980s, in her early 40's. I was devastated by her passing. I always looked forward to seeing her every summer when we took our family vacations to Philly.

This dream was confusing to me. At first, I thought she was sending me a message about the terror attack and that everything would be ok, but I still didn't understand why my aunt Vicky was in the dream. I wouldn't think anymore of the dream until June of 2002, when I learned my aunt Vickie had terminal brain cancer and was given six months to live.

A few months after this dream, I had finally gotten the call I had been waiting for almost five years. I was accepted into the Police Academy and would start in February.

I was scheduled to graduate from the Police Academy on July 28, 2002, and Aunt Vicky was going to attend. My cousin, Joanne, brought my aunt down to see my mom and the rest of the family in June. As I was there visiting her, she seemed so down and defeated. I mean, who wouldn't be after such a grim diagnosis? We were all sitting outside, on my mom and dad's deck, when I went over to my aunt Vicky and gave her a hug. At that moment she said to me, "So I guess this is the last time I'll see you!" I was just shocked, stunned, and for a brief second, I wasn't sure what to say when I blurted out, "NO! I'll see you at my graduation next month, even if I have to drive up and get you myself!" She tried to smile but I could see in her face, she knew she wouldn't be here.

Then comes the day of my graduation. As I was sitting with my classmates, I looked out into the audience to see where my family was. I noticed my aunt Vicky wasn't there. During one of the speeches, I had an overwhelming feeling of dread at one of the happiest moments of my life. I wouldn't understand that feeling I had until after my graduation. Just before my graduation party at my house, that my husband threw for me, I learned my aunt passed while I was sitting on stage. It all made sense now, I felt her passing the very moment it happened. She was given six months to live and would die just six short weeks later.

So, after my party I would learn that my mom was diagnosed with non-curable cancer and she was given a life expectancy of two years. My mom knew of her diagnosis the morning I was to graduate but didn't want to ruin my day. One of the happiest days of my life would end up being one of the worst days of my life. The selflessness it took my mom to put a smile on her face for my day knowing her sister wasn't going to make it through this day and knowing she herself was going to have to battle for her own life. So, July 28, 2002, is a day that will be etched in my head forever and it was also the day that it clicked, the dream I had was my aunt Joanie telling me that her sister was being called home.

As years would pass, I would start to understand that the dreams I had were messages from those who had already passed, or was this something bigger that I didn't fully understand?

So here I was, in my mid-thirties, a full-fledged police officer. It was my first day on the job and I was just reeling from my aunts passing and my mom's diagnosis. (My dad would also be diagnosed with Parkinson's the week after my mom's diagnosis). They put me in the busiest and most dangerous district in the city at the time, and on the inside, I was an emotional mess. I decided not to go to my aunt's funeral because I was a probationary police officer and didn't want to get into trouble for missing work. Boy, that was a mistake! My FTO (Field Training Officer) was the only one I told about what was going on and he told my sergeant. Then next thing I knew, I was being pulled into the office and getting a butt chewing for not letting them know. He told me we are a family here, and family takes care of family. From that day on, this particular sergeant took me under his wing along with my FTO.

I feel bad looking back now, because I was so busy with my new career to notice that my son was seeing shadows in our house and he still didn't tell us. Between work and court, I missed out on a lot with my family. The job is very demanding both physically and emotionally. For all I know, there could have been a ghost standing right in front of me, but I was too busy and preoccupied to even notice.

After six years on patrol and two districts under my belt, I decided to put in for the crime scene investigator position that opened up. I didn't think I would get it because I was still wet under the ears only being a cop for six years. Usually, Homicide won't even look at you unless you have ten to fifteen years on and with experience as an investigator, or so I was told. So, I thought it couldn't hurt to put my name out there and the next time the position became available, maybe they'll remember my name. Well, low and behold, I got the position along with three other officers. When I signed up to become a cop, this was my ultimate goal, to be CSI. Besides, Quincy was my hero growing up.

My mom was still alive and beat the two years of life they gave her. Even though her cancer was considered non curable, she was doing very well, she is a fighter. My dad on the other hand was declining and it was getting hard for her to take care of him with her weekly chemo treatments and the couple of bone stem cell transplants she had. After a few years under my belt in Homicide, I went to the night shift so I could help care for my mom and dad during the day while my brothers and sisters took care of them in the evenings. I was just thankful I had a job that I could work a different shift. Afterall, most of our homicides happen in the dark of night.

This is where things got interesting. After working in homicide for a few years and now on the night shift, I started noticing weird things in the office. When at work, I would always work with the lights off, a candle on my desk and work under the light of my desk lamp. This was soothing to me, but it wouldn't be long that I would start to see shadows in the lab, or the sound of doors shutting. I mean when you think about it, our office is full of the personal belongings of the victims. We investigated homicides, suicides, baby deaths, fire deaths, work related deaths, suspicious deaths, and so on. That is a lot of energy that is attached to the personal belongings we bring back to the property room.

As a matter of fact, I can remember the very first incident I had in the office. When a bunch of cop's work with one another, there are always going to be pranks. I decided one night to prank one of the other officer's while she was off work. I took this butcher paper we use to wrap evidence and strung it from the ceiling to the floor and it went all the way around her desk, I drew in window frames with flower boxes and I even cut out a working door. Her desk was completely encased. I was so proud of my work and was standing back admiring it when the lights turned on. You could hear the switch get hit by a hand and hear the clicking of the switch. At first, I thought it was someone coming in but then I remembered I had the door to the office shut and you needed a key to get in. I was terrified because this was the first time anything had happened to me at work. I was used to it at the Oakland house but that was many years ago. I had put that behind me. From this point on things started to happen almost every night I worked. Shadows, footsteps, talking, and things getting knocked over.

 On another night, in particular, I was given a new partner to work with me on nights. For the first year I was alone, so I had a year under my belt of hearing and seeing things in the office. So, on this night we were sitting in the dark, with our desk lights on, looking at fingerprints when we heard a little girl giggle from my sergeant's office. My partner jumped up and said (or yelled is more like it) "Did you HEAR that?" As I still had my head down looking at the prints under my fingerprint loop I replied with a, "Yes I did."

 "You heard that, and it doesn't bother you? That was a little girl!"

 "I know, I've been hearing her for the last year but you're the first witness I have to it, so I guess I'm NOT crazy!" I replied.

He jumped up and said, "I'm outta here! I'll be back, I'm going to get something to eat, I can't be here right now!"

 I guess I was happy because someone finally experienced what I had been hearing for a year. It's scary when you first see and hear things and then people laugh at you when you tell them. Especially cops. If you want to get teased, tell another closed-minded cop you're seeing shadows and hearing noises.

 One night I was sitting alone and two homicide detectives decided to mess with me and went into the men's restroom which was right behind my desk, moved the ceiling tiles and started hitting the air vent above my desk with a broom. It worked, I ran down the hallway in a panic, it was the loudest noise I have ever heard. We all got a great laugh at it though. One thing I didn't lose after living in the Oakland house was my sense of humor. That's what kept Patrick and I going.

    I told my family the things that were going on at work and my husband told me to make sure I keep that shit at work and don't bring it home. Uh oh, was all I was thinking. It did scare me because I didn't want anything to follow me home, he had a point, we all had been through enough, but how was I supposed to stop something or someone from following me home? Although there were some weird things I noticed in our house, I always brushed it off as me being paranoid because of the Oakland house.

    One day when I got home from work, I was showing Zian my new voice recorders we got at work to record our notes on death scenes. He asked if he could play with it and I didn't see any harm in it, so I gave it to him. If I knew what he was going to do with it, I would have told him NO. His friend was spending the night and they went down in the basement, unbeknownst to me, he and his friend were trying to get EVP's on my voice recorder. Well, low and behold they got more than they bargained for.

    Zian and his friend went down into the basement and sat on the bottom of the steps while they had the house to themselves for a bit. Zian asked if they were alone and if anyone was there to make themselves known. They heard a door shut and then footsteps coming closer to them and when they played back the recorder, they heard a "Hello" and heavy breathing. They were both scared out of their wits.

    I remember Zian telling me what they did and what they heard, and he played it for me. It was a man's voice that said "Hello" and I think that was confirmation enough for me that we had spirits in this house too.

    Were we a family that just attracted spirits if spirits were around, or did we all just have "the gift" as people would say? I didn't know the answer to this and honestly, I still don't.

This wasn't something that I ran and told Patrick right away. I needed to figure out how to tell him delicately.

Meanwhile, I was seeing and hearing things at work on a nightly basis. Since there was so much activity, I decided to write down all of the experiences I was having because sometimes I would hear and see so much it's easy to forget what happened until someone does or says something that sparks a memory.

Unfortunately, Patrick would have another significant death in his life. His best friend Kenny would commit suicide. I remember Patrick calling me at work telling me that Kenny was dead, but he didn't believe it, so he wanted me to call the police department where Kenny lived to ask them if they responded to his address. When I called and told them who I was and who I worked for and I knew they couldn't give me details but I needed to know if they were currently at a friend's address investigating a death. I knew right away when the tone of her voice changed from business to empathy. She confirmed the information and gave me her condolences. My heart was shattered. Kenny was the last guy on this earth that I ever would have thought would have taken his own life. He was so funny and when Patrick and Kenny got together it was nothing but laughs and fun times.

The funeral would come and go, and Patrick was really struggling with the loss of his best friend. I remember times when Patrick had great news to share, he would catch himself saying "I have to call and tell Kenny!" It was like reliving his death all over again for him. To this very day, he still struggles over his loss.

Kenny's wife gave Patrick some of Kenny's ashes that I had put into a necklace for Patrick. She also gave him Kenny's snow suit and a tapestry of his.

A few weeks after Kenny's death, Patrick's back went out, which it did a lot after a work accident years prior. Anyway, he was laying on the couch with his dog Neo (the German Shepherd I bought him for his 40th birthday) in the living room when Neo's ears went up and he started growling as he was looking into the dining room. Patrick got up and looked to see what

Neo was growling at but all he saw was the tapestry of Kenny's sitting on the spare couch in the dining room. He lay back down on the couch with Neo and didn't think anything of it until the next night when Neo did the same thing. On the third night, Patrick heard footsteps in the dining room while he was lying on the couch with Neo, and once again, Neo's ears were straight up and he growled in the direction of the tapestry. No one was there and he was freaked out because he heard the footsteps coming from the direction of the tapestry on the spare couch.

The next morning, I sat on the couch and Patrick was getting ready like he was going somewhere. He turned to me and said,

"I'm taking Kenny home!"

"What are you talking about?" I said.

At this point, I thought he had lost his ever-loving mind. I knew he was still very depressed over Kenny but now he was talking like Kenny was standing right next to him. Patrick told me what happened the last few nights while he was holding on to the tapestry. Now he had my attention and now I understood that he thought Kenny's spirit was in our house because it was attached to the tapestry.

He proceeded to the front door, opened it, looked into the living room, and said, "Come on Kenny, I'm taking you home!" He held the door open and acted as if he were actually watching Kenny walk out of the house. He said to me, "I'll be back!", closed the door, and walked down to the car. He opened the passenger door, threw the tapestry in the car, told Kenny to get in, acted as if Kenny actually got in, told him to put on his seatbelt, shut the door, got in the driver's side, and then he drove away.

You have to understand our relationship, we are jokesters. Living in our household is like Keto and Inspector Clouseau, we are always playing pranks on one another and from day to day you never know what is awaiting around the next corner. I knew he was okay at this point, he was using his humor to get through this, as he has done our whole life. I could only imagine what he was going to say to Kenny's wife, Sue.

When he got home, he told me Kenny was safe and sound with Sue. He went on to tell me that when he knocked on the door, Sue answered, and Patrick was standing there holding the tapestry she had given him.

"What are you doing?" Sue said.

"I brought Kenny home," he told her.

"Excuse me?! What are you talking about?" she said.

Patrick walked in her house, threw the tapestry on the floor, told Kenny he was home, and then looked at Sue as he walked out the door and told her, "He is all yours," and then left.

She must have thought he had lost his mind too. Don't worry, he called her later to explain but at that very moment, he was on a mission.

I wish I could say this was the end of it, but I think I knew deep down that this was just the beginning of another episode in our lives. Since Zian had already gotten an EVP (Electronic Voice Phenomenon), I knew there was someone or something here. It seems like everywhere we move it's like living in a house with a stranger that you cannot see. It is unpredictably chilling. You never know what each day or night is going to bring or what awaits you around each corner. Literally.

Shortly after Patrick bought back the tapestry, we started to see shadows in the house. I think the very first time was when Patrick and I were sitting on the couch watching TV one night when I saw him lean toward the dining room and look into the kitchen. He didn't say anything if I recall correctly but then a few minutes later he did it again. His side of the couch sat closest to the dining room and kitchen area while my side of the couch sat closest to the front door, so I couldn't see into the kitchen. Zian and Teall's rooms were upstairs and the steps came down into the kitchen. So sometimes when they came downstairs to use the restroom, they would come down into the kitchen and round the corner to the bathroom. It wasn't uncommon to see a shadow and it be one of the kids, but usually, they made a lot of noise when they came down the steps. They used to sound like a herd of cattle running across a field. Half the time we thought they were falling down the steps they were so loud, well, that has happened a few times too.

After he looked into the kitchen the second time, he turned to me and said he saw a shadow come from the steps and go out the back door, but it wasn't the kids. The door didn't open, he just saw the shadow come from the steps and go to the door and disappear. He went to the bottom of the steps and called the kids down. He asked them if one of them just came down the stairs and they both said no. The look on his face had the kids concerned so they asked why. Patrick told them what he saw and that is when Zian told us he has been seeing a large shadow go up and down the steps, but it always goes into his room. Now that was a frightening thing to hear. We asked him how long he had been seeing a shadow and he said it wasn't too long, but he had been hearing footsteps and other noises before he started seeing the large shadow.

Now we started having conversations on who this could be. Was it Kenny? He was tall, he was six foot four easy. Did he not leave when Patrick bought back the tapestry? Was it even Kenny that was here in the first place? Was it my job? Did I bring a spirit home from work?

Now I'm going to have to go back a little bit and explain the number of animals we had in this house. When we moved in, we had two dogs, Indy and Jr. Indy was a mixed mutt, probably a husky, lab and Beagle mix we were told. She wasn't too big. Now Jr was an ankle biter, he was a terrier poodle mix. We had them for about four years in this house before I bought Neo for Patrick. Being the German Shepherd he was, he didn't stay little for too long. Once Neo got bigger the fights between Neo and Jr started. Neo being the leader of the pack and Jr who thought he was big and bad, they tended to fight a lot. Jr usually being the aggressor and going after Neo. The day we caught Neo shaking Jr in his mouth like a rag doll, thankfully he wasn't hurt, just his pride, Indy and Jr spent most of their time in Zian's room. During this time Patrick brought home a stray cat from his work and gave it to Teall because she loved cats and she named her Church. Yes, just like the cat in the movie Pet Sematary. One day, we had all of the dogs out in the backyard when Zian tells us Indy and Neo are stuck together. Patrick is laughing hysterically and I'm yelling to get them apart because she is too old to have puppies. I know, I know, we should have gotten her fixed a long time ago, but Jr was too short to mate with her and after time had passed, I just didn't think about it. So needless to say, one day Zian called me at work a few months later to tell me Indy just had two puppies in his room. We kept one and named him Stewie, and we gave away the other one to our neighbor's friend. We didn't even know she was pregnant because she didn't show. In total, we had four dogs and a cat.

Anyway, the reason I thought this was important to fill you in on was because the animals started to react to what we were seeing. Church would just sit and stare up at the steps and hiss at nothing. Indy and Jr would always bark and growl at nothing in Zian's room.

Then the shadows started to appear in the backyard. When Patrick and I would sit in the hot tub every night before we went to bed, we would let Neo and Stewie outside to run and use the restroom. Neo would run up and down the fence line like he was chasing something. We would always brush it off as just another animal or a stray cat until I saw a black shadow running up and down the fence line in the neighbor's yard with Neo. I yelled for Patrick to look but just then it disappeared. I saw this several times and finally, Patrick witnessed it while he was sitting in the hot tub by himself one night while I was at work.

This was terrifying yet interesting at the same time. We had a shadow figure going up and down the steps and out the back door along with a shadow figure in the backyard.

Now we had an older couple that lived next to us on one side and young newlyweds that moved in on the other side of us after the older folks that used to live there passed. Patrick and I saw Kitty outside, yes that was her name, and I was asking her if they ever had anything weird, like ghosts in their house, since they lived there for 55 years. She said, "Oh yeah! We've had a ghost in our house for as long as I can remember!" Okay, our minds were blown. We both just looked at each other in utter amazement! I was expecting her to laugh at us, to be honest. I was tired of hiding from people even if they didn't believe me. She went on to tell us that her daughter had her favorite blankie when she was little and when she would take it from her and put it on the kitchen table it would suddenly disappear. She said her daughter wasn't tall enough to reach it, so she knew she didn't take it. One day, in particular, she said the blankie went missing and she said she yelled to the ghost, "You better put that blankie back by the time I come back in this room because if it isn't, there is going to be hell to pay!" Kitty said she was shocked when she came back in the room a while later and the blankie was back on the table. She told us it still lives with them and they have an understanding. Well then, it looks like we needed to take a page from her playbook.

It wasn't too long after this that Zian came downstairs and told me there was a little girl in his room. At first, I thought maybe he meant a real human being, so I asked him, "Why is there a little girl in your room?" He then said there was a little girl hiding under his desk and she was a ghost. Okay, okay you have got to be kidding me, right?! I mean that's what I was saying in my head as I was trying to process what he just told me. I asked him "You SAW a little girl under your desk just now? Like right now? How many times have you seen her?"
Zian then said, "Well when my buddy came over the other day, he told me there is a little girl that follows him everywhere he goes, but I didn't see her, but when he left, I guess she decided to stay here because she is in my room hiding under my desk!" I immediately had a flashback of the Oakland house when he told us there was a lady in his room. I could feel the blood leave my face and it felt like pins and needles were sticking me all over my body.

Of course, I went up to his room with him to see if I could see her, and I couldn't see anything. Big shocker, right? Even though I couldn't see her, I could feel her, and by that, I mean I had goosebumps all over my body and my hair was standing on end like there was an electric field around me. Zian has always been able to see spirits since he was born as far as we know, so I didn't doubt him for one second, especially after what we all went through at the Oakland house.

My biggest concern was telling Patrick, and what his reaction was going to be, because I still hadn't told him about the EVP Zian and his friend captured. Also, how do we get this little girl out of his room? Do we have his friend come back and get his little friend and he can take her back home? I wanted to call Jenny and Joe back, the ones that cleansed the Oakland house, but I lost their number years prior. I tried looking them up, but I just couldn't find them.

From this moment on the activity in our house spiked, we all noticed it, except for Teall. She has never seen anything in the house and used to laugh at us when we would share the experiences we were having. I think she thought we were all crazy and rightly so, I guess. She thought we were all paranoid. Since she wasn't born yet when we all experienced the hauntings in the Oakland house and the house was cleansed before she was born, she obviously doesn't remember anything negative in that house. She was about five years old when we moved from there and she doesn't have much of a recollection of living there. The only thing I can come up with for the reason Teall can't see the things we do goes back to the Oakland house when Jenny had me stay outside while they cleansed the house, because I was pregnant with her and her soul was pure. She did tell me that she feels safer when her bedroom door is shut since her room was right across the hall from Zian's. She said when her door was open, she always felt uneasy. So maybe she is sensitive too, but just on a different level. She can feel the spirits, but she just hasn't seen them like the rest of us. She has also heard things she couldn't explain but never really gave it much thought that it could be paranormal.

We did eventually tell Patrick about the little girl and the EVP and he reacted exactly the way I thought he would. He said Zian's buddy better come back and get the little girl or we're moving. This got me thinking, moving will never be an option for us. In three of the last four places we lived, we had activity. So, in my mind, we will never escape it. It will either follow us or if there are spirits in the next place, they would most likely try to communicate. It also had me wondering if the little girl in Zian's room was in fact from his buddy, or was this the little girl I had heard giggling in the office, and she followed me home, because now that I thought about it, I hadn't heard her at work for a while. This I kept to myself because I didn't want to be blamed for bringing something home. In reality, I don't think anyone is to blame. If you're sensitive, you will attract spirits that are looking to communicate. They will attach to you and will follow you.

Thankfully through all of this our sense of humor stayed intact. As a matter of fact, I think it just made it stronger and maybe a little darker.

One day Teall went down to the basement (which always creeped her out anyway) to do laundry and she didn't know her dad was down there in his work room. While she was loading the washer with clothes, Patrick stood around the corner, and in a very sinister raspy whisper he said, "GET OUT!". Well, she was gone. She dropped the basket of clothes and ran up the steps. She wasn't too happy with him for that although he was laughing so hard, he had tears rolling down his face. This is one of the few reasons we never won the "Parent of the Year" award. She eventually forgave him when her heart started beating again.

The activity picked up so much in Zian's room that he started to record the things that were happening on his cell phone, but the activity wasn't limited to his room, it was now spreading throughout the house.

One day Patrick and I were wrestling in the living room, this was shortly after Kenny died, and Zian was recording us. There was a moment in the video when Patrick went to grab me and I ducked, just as I ducked, an orb was flying right towards my face and it went over my head and back as I bent over. Zian saw it on his phone as he was recording it and couldn't wait to show us what he caught. Most people will say it's dust, but the difference between dust and an orb is that an orb moves with purpose. This thing came out of the ceiling and went right for us and swooped back up toward the ceiling. It almost looked like it was playing with us. Maybe Kenny? I don't know but we would ALL start catching orbs in our videos, not all of the time but a lot. If we saw the dogs or the cat reacting to something we couldn't see, we would start taking videos and taking pictures to see if we would catch anything, and to our amazement, we did.

I decided to try this at work. I had a new partner on the night shift, and he was also starting to experience the shadows and the sounds like I was. He was much more open to it than my previous partner, so we started taking videos and pictures in the dark and we caught more orbs than we expected. One thing I learned while taking videos in the dark is to have the flash or light off on the cell phone because it will pick up every dust particle known to man and orbs move in a very deliberate way. They form out of nowhere and can disappear into thin air or go into an object. There was one night when we both saw a light in the lab fly across the ceiling into the property room area. This was not an orb but more like a ball of light that could be seen with the naked eye. We both confirmed to one another that we both saw it. We looked around and saw the property room door was open when that door was always kept locked because we had money, drugs and guns stored in there along with other evidence. I know other people were experiencing things in the building too but didn't discuss it because they feared being made fun of.

The two desk Officers that worked the second and third shift always talked of the elevator doors opening up on the fifth floor when no one was in the building. The elevators in that building had to be prompted to come up to the fifth floor because it was a police facility, our homicide office. You had to be buzzed in at the front door or if you worked there you had to punch in a code to get in. Both ladies said they were so used to it that they would just say "Hello" when the doors opened because no one was there, and no one was in the building. Sometimes, that is just what you have to do to make yourself at ease. I also witnessed this for myself when I was working the desk. I heard it moving and was watching the floors as it started on one and passed each floor until it got to the 5th and the door opened with no one on it.

The rumor in the building was that a maintenance man died in the elevator shaft, he fell to his death when he was working on it. I was never able to confirm that, but people would get stuck on those elevators at least once a week. This building was built in 1913 and carries a lot of history with it.

Sometimes when I'm off work, I like to work off duty details for extra money when we're going on a family vacation or just extra play money. My favorite detail to work was SG cemetery, it is the third largest cemetery in the country. Most of the shifts were late at night which were my favorite because it was creepy and beautiful at the same time. There is just something about being in a cemetery at 3 am and watching all of the wildlife come out. It was full of deer, fox, swans, racoons, turtles and one of my favorites, skunks. Now some people might be asking why in the world does a cemetery need a cop to drive around in the middle of the night. Well, believe it or not, people would sneak in there at night and steal the copper vases on graves and illegally hunt and fish.

On one particular day I was working there I decided to bring my new camera to practice taking pictures. The cemetery had just closed, and I was the only person left inside. It was dusk on a cold December day, the ground, trees, headstones and lakes had a fresh covering of snow. It was perfect for picture taking and absolutely breathtaking. One of my favorite places in the cemetery is a road between two lakes. After I made my rounds to make sure everyone was out, I went to my favorite spot and snapped a few pictures of one of the lakes and the fresh blanket of snow that covered it.

When I got home, I downloaded the pictures on my computer and quickly glanced through them. They were beautiful.

A few years later the cemetery was having a calendar contest, so I decided to enter it and chose the picture between the two lakes. When you entered the contest, you had to post the pictures on their Facebook page so people could vote on them. I also posted the pictures to my personal page when one of my friends posted on my picture, "I hope you weren't alone when you took that picture!" I had no clue what she was talking about until I looked at the picture very closely. Oh, my Lord, there was a shadow of a lady right next to the lake. I was absolutely shocked. When I took that picture, it was so cold outside that I just rolled down my window to my cruiser and snapped a few photographs. There is absolutely no way that shadow was mine and it certainly wasn't the shadow of a tombstone, because there isn't any in that area that could cast a shadow. Besides, there was another lake directly behind me. I must have stared at that picture for hours and just thought to myself, how in the world did I miss that? She was just standing there, and it looked like she was holding a purse or a bag of some sort.

The next time I worked at the cemetery, I tried to recreate that photo. I never could. I went on my days off at the same time of day and never got a shadow in that spot. To this very day, I still take pictures there even though they planted a tree in that very spot I got the shadow. Now that's not freaky.

Oh, and by the way, that photograph didn't win the calendar contest, but it was a big hit on my social media page. I still repost it every now and again and spark some good conversations over it. I have hundreds of photographs from every season from this cemetery. I've never been able to catch another shadow figure, but the pictures are stunning, nonetheless.

Things like this get me thinking. Why is it I see and hear things not only at home and work, but now in a cemetery? Do I have a gift? Do spirits try to connect with me and my family? Are we all sensitive with the exception of our daughter Teall? This isn't limited to when I'm awake, I also have the dreams that come true eventually in one way or another. For example, one morning I was asleep, and I was having a dream that Patrick was at my mom and dad's house. He was opening every cabinet door in their kitchen and when he got to the very last cabinet above their stove he said, "So that's where you hide the red grapes," and pulled out a bag of red grapes, from the cabinet, not the refrigerator where they belong. Just then my phone rang and woke me up, it was my mom, and she said, "Hi Lynn, I was just wondering if you could run to the store and pick up a bag of red grapes for Dad? He's craving them right now and I don't have any left!" I dropped the phone on the floor with my mother on the other end. When I picked it up, she asked what that noise was, and I just explained to her I just woke up and dropped the phone and I would get some grapes for Dad.

I honestly don't even remember driving to the store, getting the grapes and driving to my mom and dad's house. I was in such deep thought and couldn't even fathom that that was possible. What does this mean? I told Mom what had happened, and I had to gently grab her jaw off of the floor and shut her mouth. I mean, what am I supposed to do with this? When I tell people about this, it blows their mind just as much as it did mine.

Now, something similar happened to me, but I was awake. I was at the store and I was walking by the lunch meat counter and saw some pickle loaf. I kind of chuckled when I saw it, because I remember thinking, people still eat this stuff? It immediately sparked a memory of my grandmother and how she used to make us a pickle loaf sandwich on dark rye bread, swiss cheese and mustard. When I got home, I scrolled through Facebook while eating my lunch when I saw a post from my friend, and this is what it said:

"Pickle loaf, Swiss and American cheese, with a little mustard, on dark rye bread…...that's what's up!"

I couldn't believe my eyes. What in the world is going on? I couldn't send her a message quick enough to tell her and she was in awe, just as much as I was.

The only thing I could think of doing was to go on the internet and search what this meant. Every time it brought me to Clairvoyance, which means "clear seeing". It's your sixth sense or intuition when you feel certain things, like a gut feeling. All police officers will tell you to follow your gut instinct, when something doesn't feel right, then it isn't. When I first came to the Police Department every veteran officer always said, "Trust your gut!" and I live by those words every day I go to work.

One night another officer and I were dispatched to family trouble back when I was on patrol, and when we got to the house, we were in the living room listening to the complainant. I had this horrible overwhelming feeling. It felt like the walls were coming in on me and I thought any minute I was going to have a panic attack. That has never happened to me, EVER! It felt like pure evil in that house. Something was wrong and I just wanted to get out, when I told the complainant, "Let's talk about this outside." Once we were outside, I felt like a weight lifted off of my shoulders. When we were finished my partner said, "What's wrong, Lynn? You look like you saw a ghost!" I told him I just needed to get out of that house because I literally thought I was going to get sick, when he said, "You know where we were at don't you? That is where the two-undercover officers were murdered a few years ago. We were standing right where they were killed!"

I almost lost my lunch when he told me that. I knew they were killed in that neighborhood before I became an officer, but I had no clue where it had happened. Their pictures were hanging in our district and I saw their faces every day. I know that wasn't the same family that lived there when this tragedy happened, but it felt like the evil from the person that took their lives still existed in that house. Afterall, he took his own life just as officers were about to apprehend him.

I knew exactly what the old timers meant when they told me to trust my instinct from that point on. Even though I wasn't in immediate danger, I felt the evil that existed in that house. It took me weeks to shake that off and I was happy when I never had to go to that house ever again, because a year later I was transferred to Homicide.

Now after nights like that, it's always wonderful to come home from an exhausting shift and soak in the hot tub before going to bed. I could never come home after processing a homicide scene and just go to bed. My mind was always racing, wondering if I missed anything, basically going through the whole crime scene in my head, hoping we got everything. Since my husband had a bad back, the doctor suggested we get a hot tub for him to soak in. We did just that. Not only was it good to relax the muscles in his back but it also helped me unwind after a long night at work. It helped me turn my brain off.

One night, in particular, I was soaking in the hot tub around three o'clock in the morning when I heard a loud bang from the neighbor's balcony. I jumped up and looked, only to see a large shadow running back and forth on their porch. At first, I thought they had an intruder trying to get in their house. As I was looking at it, I noticed I could see right through it. It was taller than their door and was running from one end of the balcony to the other. I knew right then this was nothing living, it had to be a spirit, a ghost or whatever you want to call it. I was probably only in the hot tub for about five minutes when this happened and before you know it the hot tub shut off. The hot tub cycle runs for seventeen minutes and I must have been watching this thing for at least twelve minutes. That twelve minutes felt like one. I couldn't believe what I was seeing and for how long I was seeing it. Usually, from past experiences, shadow figures tend to show themselves for a split second and then disappear.

So now I'm thinking, not only does Kitty have a ghost, and we have a ghost, but they have one too?! What in the world is going on? Is this land haunted? How many houses on this block are haunted?

I grew up just a few blocks away from here and I know this land used to be all farmland back in the late 1700s. This community was established in 1789.

We also found out there used to be a creek that ran through our backyard. We found this out when we were digging out back one day and kept hitting large rocks. Patrick was talking to Kitty's husband when he told us about the old creek bed that ran through all of our yards and that there was an Aquaphor under our property that runs down to an old spring house about a quarter mile down the street. It was built in 1790 and was a place to keep things cool and a good resting place for travelers. The spring house still stands to this day and is in remarkable condition.

From some of my research about the paranormal, I do know that some paranormal investigators believe that water and limestone is a conduit to the paranormal. Now I don't know how true that is, but I do find it interesting that there used to be a creek bed in our backyard, and we have an Aquaphor somewhere under our property.

So, after finding out this information we were talking to our neighbor and good friend that lives a couple of doors up from us, and told her about the activity we had been having, (Oh, and by the way, I still hadn't told Patrick about the shadow figure I saw on the neighbor's porch at this point) when Fran told us that their house is haunted too. She told us that she always puts her robe on the back of her bathroom door, and it went missing for about a month. She tore the house apart looking for it and couldn't find it anywhere. She said she was home alone and upstairs looking for the robe when she became fed up and yelled, "You better put my robe back or I'm gonna burn this bitch down!" She said the next day her robe was hanging back where it always did. That's exactly the same thing Kitty had happened to her daughter's blankie.

Fran also told us that her office is upstairs and the bedrooms where her kids used to sleep (they are all moved out now) are guest bedrooms, and she noticed on many occasions an impression of a body in the bed spread. She said she would straighten out the bed and the next day when she would go up there, it looked as if someone was sleeping on the bed again and left another impression. The scariest part of all of this for me is not being able to see what you're dealing with. You are literally sharing your home with a stranger. Fran pretty much has the same activity we have in our home and her immediate neighbor, Ann, also has activity.

This is five houses in a row that have paranormal activity that we know of. The houses up from Ann's house are multifamily units and we never met anyone up there, so I don't know if they experience what we do. So now it has us wondering if it's the land our houses are sitting on or if it's something else. What that something else could be, I have no clue.

Shortly after we find this out, Patrick is sitting in the hot tub by himself one night while I was at work and he saw exactly the same thing I did on the neighbor's porch. Usually when I get home from work, he is already asleep, but this night when I got home, I noticed EVERY light was on in the house and he was just sitting on the couch smoking a cigarette looking frazzled. I asked him what he was still doing up when he told me what he saw. Not thinking, I blurted in excitement, "I saw the exact same thing last week," and went on to tell him how it was running back and forth. He looked quite mad for a minute when I realized I hadn't told him what I saw, but I didn't tell him because every time Zian and I tell him something we saw or heard, he wants to put the house up for sale. I get it, but Zian and I never felt threatened. We just don't feel like whatever is here is evil. Now I admit, it is eerie knowing you're sharing a house with something you can't even see. I think at this point we have accepted our "gift", but Patrick hasn't, and Teall just doesn't see anything, my husband's daughter, my step-daughter Dev, doesn't see anything either when she is here. Half the time when Zian and I are talking about our experiences and he walks in he says, "I don't want to hear it."

## Chapter Nine

## Invisible Strangers

In case you haven't noticed, Patrick is a jokester. We love to have fun. Just recently for Christmas he bought me a huge nerf gun (fully loaded mind you). It looked like something Rambo would have used, it was HUGE. The next thing you know, he'd whip out his own gun he hid behind the couch and we would be in a full-fledged nerf war gun fight. Zian ran upstairs and grabbed his nerf gun and we were running all over the house shooting the heck out of one another. The dogs were going crazy barking at us and trying to eat our discharged nerf ammunition. It was great, a Christmas for the record books. This is a good distraction for all of us, but as soon as we have one of these days where we're having a nerf gun war, the activity picks up tenfold. I don't know if we are "disturbing" our invisible roommate or if he just doesn't have a sense of humor, but the last time I checked, this is our house now and I'm not leaving or walking on eggshells to appease him. I'm to the point now where I talk to him, and I say, "him" because the shadows we see are tall and in the shape of a man. I don't believe this is the little girl we're dealing with.

One day I was doing laundry. I had one load already in the washer and was moving them to the dryer, when the empty clothes basket, three feet behind me, hit the floor with force. I glanced over my shoulder and saw the three-foot-tall clothes basket laying on its side, about two feet from where it was sitting. Without missing a beat, I turned back around and continued loading the dryer and I said, "I'm not picking that shit up!" I was furious and at the same time, I surprised myself. I think I got to the point in my life that I have accepted that this will always be a part of my life for as long as I'm on this earth. I always thought if this happened to me here, like it did in the Oakland house, I would have run like I did back then.

I also think I have the occasional visitors too, from special people in my life that have passed on. They stop in and make themselves known on special dates or occasions and then leave again. Just make their presence known, you know, just to pop in and say hello.

On a night I will never forget, Patrick and I were getting ready to go out to dinner for our 25th Wedding Anniversary. While Patrick was in the shower, I was laying on the bed, thinking of one of my best friends that had passed away. I was just lying there, crying, and thinking about how much I missed him. The date of his passing is the day before our actual anniversary and we were celebrating a day early due to our work schedules, so this was indeed Frank's anniversary. So, as I'm lying there, the hall light in front of our bedroom came on. I looked up in confusion because Patrick was still in the shower, Zian was upstairs, and Teall wasn't home. As I was looking at the light, it went off, and then I heard Zian say, "I'm coming," as if I just called him, only I didn't.

His hall light was already on upstairs but when he rounded the corner from his room, the light in the upstairs hallway just turned off. By this time, I was in the hallway by my bedroom staring up at the light in front of my door. I looked over at him halfway down the steps leaning over the banister. "Did you see that? My light just turned off by itself!" As he reached for the light switch to turn it back on, it turned on by itself. We both looked at each other like two deer staring in the headlights. I told him it was Frank's anniversary and I was crying because I was thinking of him when the light turned on and then turned back off. I said, "Frank? Is that you? If that's you, can you turn the hall light back on?" Just then, the light came back on. I pushed my luck and asked if he could turn it back off, and off it went. Zian and I were giddy with excitement by this time. I was just happy Frank was reaching out to me. When Patrick got out of the shower, he opened the door and asked what all of the commotion was about, so we told him. Patrick knew how much Frank meant to me and didn't panic at that moment. I think he was genuinely just happy for me. This was different. We KNEW who this was and why he was here.

I am going to need to go back a bit and explain the relationship between Frank and I, but this means I will have to go back to my days as a restaurant manager.

The very first day I met Frank, he was coming in for an interview. He would have been 44 years old at the time and I was 28. When he came in, he told one of my employee's he was there to see me for an interview. When I saw him, I thought to myself, there is no way that man is going to fit in here, all of my employees were young teenagers and most had a rough upbringing, not always the easiest teenagers to work with. Frank looked a little rough around the edges even though he was dressed in a nice Polo shirt with a pair of jeans and nice shoes. He looked like he had had a rough life too. I would have never pegged him for a 44 yr. old man, he looked older to me. Anyway, we had just had our after-school rush and the lobby was trashed as it usually was. I went over to him and told him I would be running a bit late for the interview because I needed to get the restaurant straightened up. Part of me was hoping he would just leave, I hate to say that, but if I'm being totally honest, that's how I felt and I'm not proud of that. The next thing I know I see Frank wiping down tables, sweeping the floor and then he grabbed the mop bucket and just started mopping. I was floored. I knew right then, at that very moment, I was hiring this man. I felt so bad for judging him by his looks. My instincts were totally wrong, and I was ashamed of that. I was judging this book by its cover, something I was always taught not to do.

After we both got the lobby, all cleaned up, I sat down with him. I wanted to know his story. He was a Vietnam vet and he suffered from PTSD and recently separated from his wife due to his illness. Back then, you didn't hear much about PTSD and not many people knew what it was about. It just wasn't talked about back then. Well, needless to say, I hired him on the spot. To this day he was my best hire ever.

Frank wanted to work nights as a closer, which was perfect, because I needed a closer and I worked that shift a lot because my kids were younger then. When we worked together, after I would lock the doors, I would sit on the sink in the restroom while he was sweeping and mopping, and we would just talk. He was kind of like a dad to me because this is when I was going through the horrors of the Oakland house. I would talk to him a lot about it. He was always a good shoulder to lean on, full of wonderful advice. Frank and I became very close, best of friends in my book.

Frank and I had worked together for about a year, and we were due for a big inspection of the restaurant. My store manager was on a sabbatical and I was in charge of the place in her absence. I had worked for almost a full month without a day off and when I finally got a day off, one of my crew called off sick that was supposed to unload the truck the next day. If I couldn't find a replacement, I was going to have to do it. All I wanted to do was to enjoy just one day off with my family. I asked Frank if he could do it for me the next day. He told me he really didn't want to do it, but I gave him my puppy dog eyes and he reluctantly told me he would, but for me only.

As we were working the rest of our shift together, I wanted to tell Frank some big news I just got. After I locked the doors, we went to the vestibule and smoked a cigarette when I told him I was getting promoted and would be transferred to another store. He didn't take the news well. He told me if I was leaving, he was leaving. I told him not to do that, but he said, "Well, my job is done here!" That one sentence has sat with me for 24 yrs. now.

The next day, my day off, I got a call from one of my managers screaming and crying on the other end. All I could make out was that Frank died while unloading the truck and one of the managers was giving him CPR in the freezer. I jumped into my car and raced to the store and as I pulled in, the ambulance was rushing him to the hospital.

I went directly to the hospital and stayed there all night. A lot of my managers and crew were up there with me. I blamed myself. This is probably one of the hardest parts for me to write. The doctor told us to go home because there was nothing we could do for him sitting there, and to come back in the morning when they knew more.

The next morning, I was there. When I walked into his room he was hooked up to a bunch of machines and unconscious. I sat at his bedside holding his hand and I was talking to him when the nurse told me he couldn't hear me. I didn't care. I told him how sorry I was and that it was all my fault and when I looked up and saw a tear coming from his eye and rolling down the side of his face, I showed the nurse and she said that it was nothing. Well, her bedside manner was about as good as Nurse Ratchets.

The next day I came back, and his daughter was there, she said to Frank, "Your buddy Lynn is here," and his heart rate on the monitor started to go crazy. It scared me because he was still unconscious, and I thought he was having another heart attack. She smiled and told me his heart rate only does that when they mention my name. I didn't know if that was a good thing or a bad thing.

I went there every day, and on the tenth day when I showed up his bed was empty and all of the flowers, balloons, and cards were gone. When I frantically asked the nurse where he was, I could tell by the look on her face he was gone. She said, "No one told you? Frank passed away last night!" That statement sent a shockwave right through my very core. The guilt and physical pain that I felt in every cell in my body is something that I can't even put to words. I did indeed kill my best friend, at least those were the thoughts that were going through my head at that very moment. I know better now, but it took a very long time to get to the place I'm at now.

His funeral would follow a few days later and I took my ten-year gold necklace I got from my work and wrapped it around his hands in the casket. I would be riddled with guilt for many years to come. He was only 45 years old.

On the anniversary of his death, I realized, Frank and I were sixteen years apart in age, it was now sixteen years later to the day and I was now 45. He was coming back to tell me that it's okay, and I needed that. He knew I needed that.

People have told me over and over again that Frank's death was not my fault, but it didn't matter how many times they told me, I still felt riddled with guilt.

Even though Frank and I were great friends, he never shared with me that he had a bad heart. I would have never asked him to unload a truck for me if I had known. That was a disaster waiting to happen. He unloaded the truck for me hundreds of times and never had a problem. He was a strong man and looked physically fit.

When I saw where he was buried it freaked me out even more. If you drew a straight line from the Oakland house to the cemetery (which was only one street away) he was buried in, his grave was right at the rod iron fence, right up front. Of all the places he could have been buried, he was in a straight line from my house that I lived in at the time.

This is the only time Frank has ever given me a sign or came to visit me. To this day I have never seen him in my dreams or had any other visits that I can remember. That's why one of his last words to me still sticks with me today, "Well, my job is done here!" It's like he knew he was leaving me. I almost feel like he was an angel sent from heaven to set me on the right path. Afterall, he was my biggest cheerleader among my friends when I told him I wanted to follow my dreams to become an officer. Maybe angels really are sent down from heaven. I don't know, but not a day goes by that I don't think of him or talk to him. His picture is taped right below my keyboard at my office, so I can see him every day, not to mention the tattoo I got in honor of him.

This did brighten my evening as Patrick and I went on our anniversary date, and even though he stopped by for a visit, the taunting in our house continued from the strange spirit living with us.

Half of the time we learned of the things going on in our house while we were gone through Zian and his posts on social media. Here are a couple:

"The hall light in my house keeps coming off and on. Kinda freaked out!"

"Ok, I went downstairs to see what in the hell the cat was meowing about. I looked over the banister and saw the basement light was on, I walked down the rest of the steps, turned the corner and the damn lights were out!! Then I heard someone "Shush" the cat!! No one was home but dad and his ass was sleeping. Now I'm hearing a male voice….so freaked the fuck out!!!!!!"

Needless to say, it would always spark conversation with his friends but it was always unnerving for us to see this, because we never knew what was awaiting us when we arrived back home, and of course every noise Patrick heard was a ghost.

I'm the one that usually tried to explain things or debunk them, because not every sound made is due to paranormal activity. There were sometimes very good explanations. I mean, right before our furnace died it used to make some god-awful noises and every time it kicked on it sounded like there was a monkey swinging from the pipes. One of our dogs liked to sleep by the front door and when he would lay down, he would throw himself against the wall and we would hear a loud thud on our bedroom wall, and Patrick would always jump up and say, "Did you hear THAT?" I would always just say in my half awaken state with a mumble, "It's just the dog, Patrick!" and he would usually come back with, "Are you sure?" and then I would say, "YES Patrick, it's just the dog!"

This is how paranoid you become when you're living with an invisible stranger in your home. It makes you wonder if every bump in the night is a ghost, but it's when you cannot explain the noise, the voices and the shadows that make the hair on the back of your neck stand up. Those are the things that become truly frightening.

I can remember one night when the activity was really just nonstop for me at work and at the same time for Patrick at home. I don't know if there was a full moon or what but we both had experiences in two separate places.

While I was at work, I was walking out of the office into the hallway where our interview rooms were, when I saw my boss looking confused. She was peeping her head in the interview room and then walked over to the other interview room and looked inside it. She looked terrified so I said,

"What's the matter, boss? You look like you just saw a ghost."

"I think I did!" she said and then she took off without another word or an explanation.

Later she came up to my office to explain to me what happened. She told me they were getting ready to interview a woman that was the victim of a rape, so she was going to watch her investigators interview her. She turned on the monitor and saw a female with long blonde hair sitting with her head down and the lights off in the interview room. She was confused, so she switched to another monitor when she saw the woman they were actually interviewing and when she switched the monitor back to the other room, the female with long blonde hair was gone. That's when she came up to the 5th floor to look for herself, hence when I saw her in the hallway, looking confused.

Later that same evening I was working on prints when I felt a weird energy in the room and as I looked over to our AFIS (Automated Fingerprint Identification System) room, I saw a shadow peeping out of the room and it hurriedly jerked back when I looked over. It was like it was spying on me. The room was about four feet by eight feet with only one way in, through the door the shadow was peeping out of.

Apparently, I wasn't the only one having a busy night with the ghosts. Patrick was seeing the shadow man going up and down the steps almost all night while I was at work. He said it looked like it was distressed. Usually, you will catch it out of the corner of your eye just coming down the steps just once, but not all night long. Then he was hearing a man's voice and it sounded like he was having a conversation with someone. He knew it wasn't Zian or Teall because they were at work, but it was coming from Zian's room, so he decided to leave and go to a friend's house. Poor Patrick hated being home alone at night and the kids and I worked in the evenings, so he put a lot of miles on his car and motorcycles just driving so he didn't have to be home alone.

Pretty much, this is our life now. There is no sense in running from it because no matter where we go, if there are spirits there, we will see, hear, and feel them. I know some people won't understand this, but as time goes by it does get a little easier. Well, maybe not for Patrick, but I have noticed a little change for the better, except for when something major happens, like the time Zian showed us a video of the Darth Vader light we got him for Christmas turning off and on by itself. As soon as it started to happen, he pulled out his phone and videotaped it. He was sitting in his bedroom and he was commentating on how he is sitting about three feet away from the light when it turned on, so he showed his hands and showed where the switch was when it turned back off. He said, "Look, I aint even touching it! Look, it's back on!" This went on for about thirty seconds.

Another video he took was also a night he was home alone. He had just finished his chores, which was cleaning the kitchen. He went up to his room when he was finished to play some video games when he heard a loud clanking noise in the kitchen sink. He got his cell phone out and recorded himself in his bedroom and said,

"I'm up here in my bedroom, home alone, and I heard a loud noise in the kitchen. It sounded like something fell in the sink. I'm going to head downstairs and see what it was."

He started down the hallway steps and walked around the kitchen and everything was nice and tidy. He went over to the sink was stunned to see the lid to the cork holder in the sink. He explained how to his audience how the cork holder sits on the windowsill above the sink and showed how the lid snapped on. He also showed how it just doesn't come off without some force and that even if it wasn't pushed all the way in, there was no way it could fall on its own. He then picked up the lid and dropped it in the sink to show how loud it was when it hit the metal. The lid is also made of metal and it has some weight to it.

I could tell things had moved up a notch, now things were moving in the house, and the clothes basket was my first experience. I have had another occasion where after I went grocery shopping and put everything away, I sat down to watch TV. The dogs and cats were all huddled in the living room with me when I heard a soft thud in the kitchen. I sat there really still for a second with the hair on the back of my neck standing up. I went in to investigate when I found the new loaf of bread, I just bought, sitting right smack in the middle of the floor. No, I didn't leave it on the edge of the counter, and it didn't just fall. I always put my bread up against the wall, so it stays nice and cool and the counter is about two and a half feet wide. We all know what gravity is, and if I had set the bread on the edge and it fell, it would have fallen straight down and landed by the cabinet. It would have had to roll about four or five times to get to the middle of the floor.

    As all of this was going on, my dad's health was deteriorating quickly with his Parkinson's. Mom had broken her femur trying to step over her cat, and it was getting hard for her to take care of Dad. It wasn't until she was in the hospital that we realized just how bad he was. He couldn't even take the foil off the top of his yogurt and needed help getting dressed.

    Since I was working the night shift, I would go to their house after work and spend the night. Between my brothers and sisters, we would all take shifts staying with them through the day and through the night. This was an eye opener for all of us, on how bad our dad was doing, and to think Mom was trying to take care of him all by herself all the while she was dealing with her cancer and having weekly chemo infusions. She was weak and tired and needed time to rest from her own disease. This is hard on a young adult, much less a woman in her seventies, but that generation is so different, they do not ask for help. They believe their problems are just that, their problems, and don't reach out for help. Since I worked nights and all of my brothers and sisters worked day jobs, I would do Mom and Dad's grocery shopping. Sometimes three times a week, because Mom "always" forgot something each day I went. This was exhausting on all of us. Not only were we working our jobs, taking care of our families, but we were taking shifts to take care of Dad while Mom was recovering from a severe break in her leg.

    My sister Diane worked for a facility that did home health care for the elderly. Her company would be hired by families that did not want to put their mother's, father's, husbands, and wives in nursing homes. She wanted to meet with all of us to pitch the idea of moving Mom and Dad into her and her husband's home and take care of them like she did with so many strangers in her day to day. We all had mixed feelings, but at the same time none of us wanted to see them in a nursing home, but we all knew this wouldn't be a nine to five job, it would be a 24/7 job. It's not like you can just punch a timecard and be done with it, they are living with you and would need care all of the time. Mom wanted to pay Diane what she was making at her job and ultimately, this is what we all decided upon, and we would all pitch in to help Diane the best we could.

It was decided that this is what we were going to do, so Diane's husband, Tony, who is a contractor, made some modifications to their home to get it ready to move Mom and Dad in. This was the most selfless act on both of their parts. This would be a big change for them, because not only did they have four grown children, but they had a "million" grandbabies, and that is a lot to juggle. She is going to kill me for that, but I lost count of her grandchildren.

After the remodel in their home, we moved Mom and Dad in with them. It would be challenging on the whole family, but more so for Diane because this undoubtedly put a big strain on her, emotionally and physically. I would continue to do the grocery shopping since I knew what Mom wanted after doing it for so many years, and the rest would give breaks to my sister so she could relax. It was tough on all of us, and sometimes had us all at each other's throat, but we would make this work.

As all of my brothers and sisters and I were going through this, our daughter had big news for us. She enlisted in the United States Marine Corps. We were so proud of her, well, her daddy was a little disappointed, because when she said she wanted to join the military, he thought she meant the Army. Patrick was in the Army, so he thought his baby girl was going to follow his footsteps. He said he was so proud and crushed at the same time because she didn't join the Army. They still kid around about who is better, the Army or the Marines. We never cried so much, watching our baby girl get on that bus headed to boot camp. There wasn't a dry eye in the car as Patrick, Zian, Dev, and I drove home. Other than the sniffling, it was the quietest ride home.

It seems like one minute your kids are in diapers, you're cutting gum out of their hair and washing the crayon drawings from the walls they so proudly drew, and the next minute they are grown adults, living their own lives. Sometimes it's a hard pill to swallow but watching them grow and make life changing decisions for themselves, is very gratifying. We couldn't be prouder of the adults our children have grown to be. You always hope and pray as a parent that the foundation you laid for your kids is good enough. I think Patrick and I did a pretty good job.

It wouldn't take long for the noises in the house to start in Teall's empty room. While she was living at home, we never heard the bumps and the bangs coming from there, like we did in the rest of the house, but now they had expanded their horizons.

Once Teall left, I would bury myself in working extra duty details so we could visit her every chance we got because we had no idea where she would be stationed once she finished boot camp. During this time, we had big changes at work too. We were getting ready to move our offices to a new building. I remember a few of us that had experiences at our old building, wondering if the activity would follow us to the new one. There wasn't a doubt in my mind that we would have the same activity in the new place. We collect way too much energy filled evidence, personal belongings of those that have passed. Pretty soon that energy would be moved to a new location. Now, we didn't know if we would bring the old energy with us or if we would create a new environment with new energy, or maybe a combination of both.

One day my boss took me to the new place while it was still being converted into a police facility, with a new lab and completely new set up from what we had at our old building. It was so exciting to see the new layout and the huge lab we were going to have to work in, along with all of the state-of-the-art equipment we were getting. The old building, we were used to working in was so old and outdated and the lab we worked in was nothing more than a tiny room. It definitely didn't live up to lab standard.

When we finally moved into our new building, the spirits wasted no time at all in letting us know they were there. The very first experience I had, I was sitting in the new office, still working the night shift, when I heard the lab door slam shut. We had key cards to get into the lab and only the criminalist and our immediate bosses had access. Our homicide detectives don't even have access to the lab. Knowing I was the only person on our floor, I went to go check it out and see who or what was in the lab.

Now this building doesn't have your typical light switches, where you turn on the light when you walk in the room, they are motion censored lights, they turn on when someone opens the door. When I got to the lab, I could see the lab lights were on, shining under the lab door. The hair on the back of my neck was standing on end as I swiped my keycard to go in. I wasn't surprised no one was in there, as a matter of fact, I expected it to be empty. I did, however, notice the property room door was open and it is always kept shut and locked. When I was in there earlier in the evening, I specifically remember it being shut.

When I went back into the office and sat down, I heard another door slam. I got up and went upstairs where the desk officer was and asked her if she had let someone else in the building. She told me, "NO! I didn't, but I have been hearing doors slamming ALL night long!" I could see she was frazzled. She said, "It's just like the old building! I knew it would follow us!" I knew this particular officer was working on the desk, as we all take turns covering it, which means buzzing other officer's in when they need to use the interview rooms, test firing weapons recovered from suspect's and dropping off property into the court property room. No one can just walk into this building. There are cameras everywhere and if you do not work here on a daily basis, you don't have access to the building. I just knew she wouldn't laugh at me when I told her what happened in the lab because she believed just as much as I did, that we had paranormal activity in the old office, and now in this one.

At this point in my career, I really didn't care if people believed me or not. In the past it was something that bothered me, but either you believe it exists or you don't. It didn't matter to me anymore, which side of the fence you were on. All I know is that my family and I have experienced this type of activity for many, many years at home and it apparently isn't any different for me at work. Either you are open or you're not.

Now back at the homestead, we got the news that Teall had passed the Crucible and was now a Marine. We couldn't wait to see her graduate. We traveled to Camp Lejeune, North Carolina to watch our Marine graduate. I can't even put to words how proud of her we were and are. The experience was an awe-inspiring experience we will never forget and soon we would have her home for Christmas before she left for Camp Pendleton, in San Diego, California.

Unfortunately, before we would go to Camp Pendleton, my grandfather would pass away. He was my Poppy and passed away a few months before his 102nd birthday. The family traveled to Philly, where he was from, for his funeral, and we stayed at my uncle's house. All of us, meaning my brothers and sisters, along with my mom stayed with them. There were blow up mattresses all over their condo. Since Patrick stayed behind to watch our dogs, Zian went with me. I was lucky and landed in a bed with my mom, instead of an uncomfortable blow-up mattress. We slept in her dad's bed, my Poppy's room. When Mom and I lay down to get some sleep before laying Poppy to rest next to my grandmother that passed many years ago, my mom and I heard three knocks on the wall. I looked over at her to see if she heard it, but she was already staring at the wall. I said, "Did you hear that, Mom?" She replied, "I did," I then said, "I wonder if that was Poppy telling us to get out of his bed!" She laughed and said, "Well, he was a prankster, so I wouldn't put it past him!" We both had a laugh and soon slipped into a deep sleep.

My Poppy was probably one of the biggest pranksters I knew. Standing all of five feet tall, this little Italian was full of laughs and jokes. When I was a little girl, I couldn't wait to travel to my mom's hometown in Philly to see my Poppy, my grandmother, my aunt's and uncle's and all of my cousins. We only got to see them once a year and visiting there made up some of my best childhood memories. Especially going crabbing with Poppy and then when we got back to his house my grandma would be ready to throw the crabs in the pot and make the best Italian dinner known to mankind.

So, while we were all sleeping the night before Poppy's funeral, every fire alarm went off in the house, waking every one of us up and scaring us half to death. I remember my uncle running out in his boxers, half asleep while the strobe lights to the alarm were flashing. As quickly as he got out of his bedroom and ran down the hallway, they stopped. After we all got our hearts beating again and checked to make sure there wasn't a fire anywhere, we all went back to bed. I think as soon as everyone was about to drift back off to sleep, they went off again. Once again, we were all scared out of our wits. These alarms were deafening and then you add the strobe light effect, we're lucky no one had a heart attack. My uncle said, "I don't know what the hell is going on, (in his thick Italian South Philly accent) this has never happened before! Ever!" Then I turned and looked at Mom and said, "I bet it was Poppy!" and she said, "I'm beginning to think you're right!"

To this day, my aunt and uncle say they can still hear him shuffling down the hallway with his walker. He still likes to play his pranks on them.

The next month, we flew to San Diego to see Teall at her base in Camp Pendleton. We were having a great time when I got a call from home, some 2,000 miles away, saying our dad fell ill and they had to put him on Hospice at my sister Diane's house. That's a hard thing to hear when you are so far away from home and there is nothing you can do. We only had a few days left, so we tried to enjoy the time we had left with Teall because we honestly didn't know when we would get to see here again.

When we got home, I wasted no time going to see my dad. He was still awake, but bed ridden, his organs were shutting down one by one. Watching your dad die slowly is one of the most painful things I have ever witnessed. I don't know how Diane did it, because they lived with her, she didn't have a break from watching him slip away.

My dad was the healthiest person I had ever met. When I was still living with my parents, I remember him coming home from work and working out in the basement and then running three to four miles every day. I don't think there was ever an ounce of fat on that man.

Watching him widdle away right in front of our very eyes was heartbreaking. Parkinson's is a terrible disease and I wouldn't wish it on my worst enemy.

It steals your mind, your memory, and your most basic motor functions. Even though my dad was a quiet man and didn't always express to us if he was proud of us or not, the Parkinson's did bring out another side to him before he got really bad.

I used to take Mom and Dad to their doctor's appointments since I was free during the day, and when I would take Dad to see his neurologist, he would introduce me to his doctor every time and say, "This is my daughter Lynn, she works in homicide, she's a crime scene investigator!" The doctor would play along like it was the first time ever meeting me and shake my hand and give me a wink. Even though he never told me personally that he was proud of me, I knew every time I took him to the doctor, he was indeed proud.

We all watched Dad deteriorate more and more each day for a month. It was horrible. Patrick decided to take me out on a date night to get my mind off of things and right after we finished a wonderful dinner at an upscale restaurant (which is something we never did), we were walking through the park downtown when my phone rang. It was my sister Diane, telling me to come to her house immediately, Dad didn't have much time left. Even though I knew I would be getting that phone call at some point real soon, you can never properly mentally prepare yourself for it. I was shaking to the very core of my soul.

Patrick took me to see my dad, he was barely holding on and unconscious. He was gurgling when he was breathing, and my sister told me that that was called the "Death Rattle." That's a horrible term and I still don't like it when I hear someone say those words, because it takes me right back to that place in time.

Our other sister Rita was out of town in Texas. We were so scared she wouldn't make it home in time to say goodbye to him. Rita was very close to Dad. We kept telling Dad that she was on her way home and because she was scared, she wouldn't make it home in time, we put the phone to his ear so she could say her goodbye's. She told Dad if he couldn't hang on it was okay to go home to be with his mom and dad. She took the first flight home and Dad was still holding on. We all took turns going into the room and talking to him. We even put some old family videos on the TV and watched them in his room, hoping he could hear the good times we had as a family.

We then took my mom to the cemetery so she could pick out his casket and headstone. Now that is an eerie thing to do when your dad is still alive but just barely holding on. I know it had to be done, but it was still very hard to do.

Then my mom asked what his plot number was because she couldn't remember it. The man behind the counter looked it up and said it's "286". I almost passed out. That is my badge number. My mom bought that plot for them when I was sixteen years old. What are the odds? I said, "Oh my God, 286 is my badge number, Mom!" Everyone had the look of shock on their faces. Of all of the numbers in that huge cemetery, his plot number was the same as my badge number. I mean, it still blows my mind every time I think about it.

The man walks us to the grave site when I look down and I see Virginia's grave. YES, Virginia, the lady in Zian's room at the Oakland house. She was buried just four plots down from my dad. Are you kidding me right now? This was something I kept to myself when we were at the grave site, but I was exploding on the inside. I'm not a "coincidence" kind of gal. I believe there is some sort of connection in everything we do, but this was mind blowing, and not to mention, Virginia died 26 yrs. before my dad.

I remember when I was sixteen years old and my mom and I were driving past the cemetery when she said, "That's where your dad and I are gonna be buried, right next to that tree!" Which I quickly responded, "Stop it, Mom! I don't want to hear about that! How morbid!" Now I think back to when I was sixteen and Mom showing me their plot, Virginia would pass just six years later, from the time my mom purchased it, and I would move in Virginia's house just eight years after Mom pointed out their grave site. It will make your head spin if you ponder on it too much.

I find it fascinating and yet creepy at the same time, that I have always wanted to be a police officer, and out of ALL of the badge numbers I could have been appointed, mine was the same as my dad's plot number and it's also the beginning of Zian's SOC number.

Once we left the cemetery, we went back to Diane's house to be with Dad. All of us kids and Mom would take turns going in to see Dad and just talk to him, pray, or say their goodbye's. I decided to crawl into bed with him, hold his hand and let him know it was okay to let go and be with grandma and grandpa and that we would all take care of Mom. She would be in good hands. I told him how much I loved him and just lay there with him holding his hand, but I told him that when he does leave us, I asked him if he could show me a sign that he was okay once he adjusted to his new life.

Later that night, we all crashed at Diane's house because we all wanted to be near in the event Dad passed in the middle of the night. I took the couch and Diane gave me the small monitor to the video camera we had in Dad's room. I was just lying there for about an hour because I couldn't sleep listening to Dad's labored breathing, when I heard footsteps around his bed, coming from the monitor. I jumped up and looked at the screen to see if anyone was in the room with him, but I knew if someone went in there, they would have to pass me first. So as my eyes were plastered to the screen, I could still hear the footsteps in his room, and then I saw two orbs materialize above my dad's head and they were moving all around his body. My immediate thought was it was my grandma and grandpa coming to take him home. I just couldn't stop watching, it seemed like it lasted a lifetime, but in reality, it was only twenty seconds (give or take) that I saw them, when they suddenly vanished.

The next day, I showed my sister Diane and my mom, their eyes were glued to my phone as they watched it. It was the most calming thing I have ever witnessed. I think it helped us all knowing grandma and grandpa were waiting for Dad.

The next evening, Dad would take his last breath with my mom and his children surrounding him, holding his hands. Dad was now at peace with his mom and dad. No more pain. Oh, how I miss him.

The next morning, I went back home and was just sitting on my back porch, when my neighbor Danielle came over with two huge margaritas and said, "You look like you could use a drink!" So, we sat with our drinks and I told her I asked my dad to give me a sign he was okay when a big blue and black butterfly flew right in between us and landed on my back door. I stopped talking mid-sentence and we both just looked over at one another in disbelief when Danielle said, "I think your dad just gave you his sign!" Then just like that, the butterfly flies right in between us again and rounds the corner between our houses and disappears. The weird thing about this butterfly was that it wasn't flying all over the place like most butterflies do. You know, they look like they are drunk just fluttering all over the place, bouncing into things with no real purpose. This one flew in a straight line, with purpose. I still believe my dad gave me my sign, and then my work sent a beautiful flower arrangement with a bunch of blue and black colored butterflies in it. I still have one of them sitting on my desk at home and a month later I would get a butterfly tattoo exactly like the one we saw and I had the words, "I'll hold you in my heart until I can hold you in Heaven." tattooed underneath it.

It was long after Dad had passed that I was sitting in my living room in silence, home alone, and just thinking about him when I heard his cough coming from my kitchen. I jumped up and ran into the kitchen and no one was there, so then I went into the basement thinking Patrick came home and came in through the garage, but he wasn't there. It was so loud.

My dad had a very distinctive cough with his Parkinson's. It was his cough. I sit in an office with eleven other people, and if someone coughs at their desk, I can tell who it is without seeing them. This wouldn't be the last cough I would hear in my house from my dad. I'm sure it was just another way of him letting me know he was here.

It took a while to get into the grind of things because I spent the last six to seven years working nights and helping out Mom and Dad along with the rest of my brothers and sisters. All of our lives were going to change now. The routines we were used to for so many years were over.

Now I was back to work and trying to get used to my new way of life without Dad in it. I took a detail at SG cemetery, you know, the one with the shadow lady I caught in the picture. Well, they were having a beer tasting event and I was standing off to the side minding my own business when out of the corner of my eye, I saw this guy walking up to me. I really wasn't in the mood to strike up a conversation, but I saw he was still coming toward me and got about three feet away from me when I turned toward him, but he was gone. There was no one there. He was solid as solid can be. There were around me but the closest one was probably twenty feet away. I was turning around and looking over my shoulders, probably had a very confused look on my face, when one of the cemetery workers approached me and said, "Did you see a ghost?" as he was chuckling. I said, "I think I did!" I continued to tell him what had happened to me and he said, "Yeah! We think he was one of the caretakers here. Only the sensitive people can see him, but he likes to walk up on people!" Then I told him about the picture I caught a few years prior, and I pulled out my phone and showed him the picture. He says, "Oh yeah! That's the Basket Lady. She walks all over the place and carries a basket. Quite a few people have reported seeing her. I've never seen a picture of her though, that's a good one you got there."

I have never felt more validated than I did at that very moment. He even told me that he is seen wearing tan overalls and a hat, and that is exactly what I saw. Although I'm not sure what kind of hat he had on because I saw him out of the corner of my eye, I could tell he was wearing one. I think this is another reason why I liked working this detail, because I just never knew what I was going to see.

Now that this year was coming to an end, I was just hoping that after losing my Poppy and then my dad, just a few short months apart, the next year would be better. On New Year's Day, Zian let Indy and Jr. outside to play, when he went to let them in, he saw that Indy had fallen into our pond. Nothing had seemed out of the ordinary when he let them out, but she must have had a medical event causing her to fall in the pond. Indy was eighteen years old, but you wouldn't have known it by looking at her, she was still full of spunk.

We brought her into the house and wrapped her in blankets and were trying to warm her up with a hair dryer, but it must have been too much for her, and Indy had a stroke. We rushed her to the vet, and we had to make the decision to let her go. It was horrible. We had her since she was a puppy. It broke my heart to see how devastated Zian was.

Now I was worried about our other dog Jr., we got them at the same time, they were best friends. I just knew he would be lost without her and sure enough, the day before Valentine's Day, just a month and a half later, Jr. had a stroke too. There was nothing we could do for him and we had to let him go to be with Indy. This was a hard blow for all of us, but especially Zian. Those dogs stayed up in his room with him and they were his best friends. Our house seemed so empty now. This year wasn't starting out the way we had hoped, but it wouldn't be long before we would hear the pitter patter of them running around upstairs in the middle of the night. Neo and Stewie would stare from the bottom of the steps looking up at Zian's room. Indy was Stewie's mother and Neo was his father, it was sad to think their family had broken apart. It makes you wonder if they knew what was going on. I think dogs are much smarter than we give them credit for.

Zian has told me that he would occasionally hear Indy and Jr. walking around his bed when he was asleep at night and I believed him, because I have heard those same noises when he is at work. They were definitely different from the sounds I hear up there from the shadow man and the little girl.

As time goes on in our house, it seems like the activity picks up. One-night Patrick and I were sleeping, and I felt and heard him getting to get out of bed to use the restroom. That seems like a common thing between the two of us now, the older we get, the more potty breaks we need. It would be a miracle if either one of us could sleep through the night without having to make a run for the bathroom. Anyway, I saw him stumbling down the hallway like he always does, so when I turned over to face his side of the bed, I was horrified to see he was still in bed with me. If he was still in bed with me then who in the hell was that walking down the hallway and why did I feel the bed move when I thought he was getting up. He was sound asleep. I even nudged him, and he didn't move. I was terrified. I know I said I was getting used to seeing the shadows, but when you feel the bed move as if something was getting out of it, that takes it to a whole new level. I tried to explain it away, like maybe I was in some state of sleep and I dreamt it.

Then a few months would pass by and the exact same thing happened again. In total, this has happened five times to date. I don't know what this means and it's driving me nuts. Is there a spirit getting into bed with us or what? And if that doesn't make one's skin crawl then I don't know what will.

About four months into the new year, my bosses decided to pull me off of nights because I was getting stagnant. To be honest, this was music to my ears. Working nights in a homicide unit means a heavy caseload, because that's when the criminals are out. I needed a break and I needed to be around people, because working nights alone gets lonely. There is no one to bounce ideas off of, you are pretty much on your own. Since my dad was gone, there really wasn't a reason I needed to work the night shift anymore, and now maybe I could spend more time with my husband, and go for those motorcycle rides out in the country after we get off of work like we used to. I was missing my family, because I was already gone to work by the time Patrick got home from work, and that in and of itself was putting a strain on us.

Another train of thought when it came to working the dayshift was, I probably wouldn't notice the activity in the office like I did when I was alone at night. Well, I guess I was wrong because it continued, but just not as often. Our office can get quite noisy with people going in and out constantly. One day another officer and I went into the lab to work on a case of ours, I got what we needed out of the property room and shut the door (which automatically locks when it shuts) when we turned around to carry the evidence over to the table. As we set the evidence down, we both turned at the same time to see the property room door opening slowly. I said to him, "I did shut that right?" and he said, "YES you did. I even heard the door latch when it closed!" Right then, he held both of his arms out to show me the goosebumps with his hair standing on end. This would be the fourth officer to experience something with me between both buildings. Another validation that I'm not losing my mind.

In that office, while working dayshift, I had my hand touched and something blew into my ear. Not a light breeze, but like someone was standing right behind me that it made my hair move. I turned around quickly, knowing no one was there because I was in the lab alone. Now I don't know if it's victims trying to get my attention or what. There are SO many victims, how could I possibly know "who" it is?

Finally, the time would come for Patrick and me to get away and go on a vacation to see my cousin in Colorado. It would be a nice break from the activity, and just life in general. Joanne and her husband, Jason, bought a B&B in Estes Park and moved their family there.

We had never been to Colorado before and it was the most magnificent and beautiful place I have ever seen. Their B&B consists of a bunch of little cabins at an altitude of 7,522' just sitting back in the mountains, with the Stanley Hotel and downtown Estes Park visible from their property. My husband even stopped a police officer there and asked him if they could hire me there. The Officer chuckled and said that they were hiring, and I could probably do a transfer. I wish he never said that, because for the next two months I would have to hear my husband beg me to move there. I wasn't about to start all over again, at that point I had already vested sixteen years to my department. Maybe that will be in our future plans after I retire, ya never know.

The first day there they took us to a little diner to eat but when we got there, the owner said his only waitress had called off sick, and since Joanne knew the owner, she started bussing tables. I couldn't let her do that alone, so of course, the next thing you know, I'm helping her, and we are serving food to tables. It was hilarious, but we ate for free.

After we finished eating, they took us sightseeing in downtown Estes Park. That place was just gorgeous, all the little shops surrounded by a large stream of water coming off of the mountains. I could just stay there and never go home. We told Joanne and Jason that I could be their housekeeper and Patrick could be their landscaper. I would just take an early retirement and do that for a place to stay. Well, it's a pipe dream because the cost of living there is much higher than where we are, but a girl can dream right.

After a long day of sightseeing and sitting by the campfire, we decided to go to bed and get ready for our next day, not to mention the altitude change was kicking our butts.

Patrick and I retired to our cabin and snuggled up in the bed and we were both out like a light. At about 3 o'clock in the morning, I was awoken by footsteps around our bed. I thought maybe Patrick got up to use the bathroom, but he was still asleep. I sat up in bed just listening. I didn't hear anything else, so I went back to sleep and brushed it off as me just hearing things.

The next day Joanne and Jason took us for a drive through the Rocky Mountain National Park. Estes Park is the eastern gateway to the National Park, and it is just stunning. There was elk everywhere. When we would wake up some mornings, there would be a herd of elk laying on their property at the B&B. What a beautiful sight to wake up to.

After another long day of just soaking in this beautiful mountain scenery, we headed back to the cabin and sat by the fire and watched the sun go down behind the mountains. The sunsets there are nothing like I had ever seen before.

After we went to bed, I would be awoken again by the sound of footsteps in the living room area along with a loud thud. This even woke up Patrick. We both just looked at each other and neither of us had to say a word. We were both thinking the same thing, we can't even escape this while we're on vacation.

The next day Joanne had made reservations for us to eat at the Stanley Hotel. I have always been intrigued by it, because I knew that is where Stephen King got his idea for the book, "The Shining", while he was staying there as a guest.

So of course, we had to do the ghost tours they had there, we live it every day, so why not check it out and see if this place really is haunted. While we were walking around the place with the tour guides and a group of people, Patrick and I were taking multiple photos in every room we went in. We didn't see anything in particular with our eyes, but Patrick snapped a few pictures down a hallway and caught a spectacular shadow figure. The first picture there was nothing there, the second picture there is a large shadow figure coming out of the hallway and entering the room we were in, and in the third photo, it is gone. We were giddy with excitement that he actually caught proof of something.

**The Stanley Hotel**

When we got back to our cabin, we were looking through the rest of the pictures, when Patrick noticed he caught the apparition of a young boy dressed in clothing from the late 1800s to early 1900s, in a doorway from the bar we were drinking in earlier. It was so cool to see. I know that sounds funny coming from me, but catching something in a picture is really indescribable, and we're not living with this one. To capture something that you couldn't see with the naked eye that was standing right in front of you is fascinating to me. I don't know why you can capture some and others elude you. We have been snapping pictures in our house for years now and have only captured orbs. We have yet to capture the shadow man or the little girl, but I'm thinking that's a good thing, because seeing his shadow out of the corner of my eye is enough for me.

After looking at all of the pictures, we headed to bed. I was lying on my back and Patrick was facing me. He woke up in the middle of the night because he felt like someone was standing over him, so he turned to look over his shoulder and as he turned back around toward me Patrick yelled, "Oh my God, watch out, Lynn!" as he threw his whole body over mine, as if to shield me from something. I was startled to my core and had no clue what was happening.

He explained to me that he felt a presence in the room looking at him and when he turned back over toward me, a shadow shot out from the closet behind me and that's when he threw himself on top of me. Needless to say, neither one of us slept for the rest of the night. I guess this is the curse of being open, sensitive or whatever you want to call it. It seems we can't even escape it while on vacation.

Besides my sister Diane, Joanne had always been one of my biggest supporters when it came to the paranormal and the experiences we have had. When we told her what happened she believed us completely. She is always the one who asks me what new ghost stories I have whenever she comes to visit me. Fortunately for us, the rest of the week went on without a hitch, and then I even had a butterfly land on my nose for about a minute. My husband was taking pictures of it meanwhile I was looking cross eyed trying to look at this beauty. I guess Dad was making an appearance, or at least I like to think that. Every time I see a butterfly, I say "Hi Dad!"

About a month after we returned home, my cousin Tom and his son Nick came over for a visit. Nick had never been to my house before and for that matter, he didn't know what was going on in our house.

Nick and I were talking and he kept looking away from me and staring into my dining room. After a few times of looking away from me, he said, "I'm sorry, I'm not trying to be rude, but that man standing in your dining room is very distracting." The chills enveloped my entire body. I knew exactly who he was talking about, only I couldn't see him. I said to him, "You can see him? What do you see?" He told me he was a very tall man and had a hat on. He said he didn't seem like an evil presence, but maybe a little irritated. I then asked Nick if he had abilities and he told me yes. He said he has had abilities since he was a child and that it ran in his family. His mother, who had just passed a month earlier, had abilities as well. I will never forget what he said to me next, he said, "There is a lot of death here. I could feel it when we pulled into your driveway. It's not the house, it's the land that it sits on." I was absolutely blown away. I wanted to see how good his skills were and invited him out to the side porch where our hot tub is. As soon as he stepped out, he looked over at the neighbor's balcony and said, "I don't get a good feeling over there. I think there is something trapped on the porch up there. He can't get out." This kid, my cousin, was blowing my mind. He nailed everything we had been going through. He then went on to tell me there was a little old man here and he laughs a lot and likes to play jokes. He also said he was very, very short and he even saved my life, but he doesn't stay here, he just likes to pop in to see how we are. I knew immediately that he was talking about my Poppy. He described him perfectly. He never met my poppy; he didn't know my mom's side of the family. There was no way he could have known this stuff. And as far as my Poppy saving my life, he was right, but that's not something I'm ready to talk about, and it is something no one knew about, not even Patrick.

Now I can say for sure that the shadow figure we had been seeing for years going in and out our back door is a man, and he is tall. It's what we have always thought, but our ability is not as strong as Nick's. I would have kept Nick here if I could have, I could listen to him for days on end. His abilities are fascinating to me and he seems to have an old soul. Very in tune with himself and his surroundings. Nick told us we could sage the house and see if that helps, and honestly, I was scared to do it ourselves, because I have heard you can mess that up and make it worse.

After Tom and Nick left, I told Patrick how Nick had read the house and saw our shadow man. We decided to sage the house and I ordered a sage kit. Once it came in, we read the directions very closely and opened every window in the house in the dead of winter and as Patrick was saging, I was following behind him reading the prayer. You could tell we were a bunch of amateurs at this. I remember thinking while Patrick and I were saying the prayer, he was yelling it like the spirits were deaf. I told him at one point "I don't think you have to yell, I'm pretty sure they can hear you." It seemed to go well because things were quiet in the house for a long time. Not a peep, no footsteps, no doors opening on their own and no lights turning on and off by themselves. It felt like the heaviness in the house had just lifted off of us. I guess Patrick's yelling worked.

It was nice to feel like we had our house back. During this time, we rescued a dog named Fenway, he was a Bavarian German Shepherd, and just a year and a half old, but about the size of a horse. He got along great with the other dogs, but we forgot to ask if he liked cats. We would find that out soon enough when he was in the house for about twenty minutes and both Marvin and Church decided to make an appearance, and Fenway knocked over every piece of furniture trying to eat them. The next time I rescue a dog I will make sure to ask if cats are on the menu. All we knew is that we needed to keep Teall's cat alive while she was in the Marine Corp. She has threatened us multiple times that she would stab us in the eye with a toothpick if anything happened to her cat. It was a crazy time for sure, it took about six months for Fenway and the cats to finally get along. It was like an episode of Tom and Jerry in our house when Spike, the American Bulldog, would chase Jerry every time he had the chance. Eventually they would bury the hatchet, and before you know it, Marvin would cuddle up next to Fenway and they would both catch some Zzzzz's.

The following year, Teall would be coming home for good, she was medically retired from the Marine Corps after three years of serving, and she would be moving back home. We were happy to have her, just not under the circumstances. She always wanted to be a lifer in the Marine Corps and hoped to one day be a drill instructor, but an MS diagnosis would cut that dream short.

About a year and a half after Teall got home, we would lose Neo. We awoke one horrible morning to find that Neo had passed in his sleep. Neo was Patrick's best friend, he was the dog I bought for him for his 40th birthday, he was Stewie's dad and he literally saved my husband's life four years before he slipped away in the middle of the night. We were grateful that we didn't have to put him down like we did with Indy and Jr. I don't think Patrick would have survived that. This house was the only home Neo knew. I don't care what anyone says, losing a pet can be as devastating as losing a family member. I have heard people say, "It was just a dog." I think that is one of the most insensitive things you could say to someone that has just lost a beloved pet.

One night while we were getting ready for bed, Patrick was holding my hand in bed and he was saying a prayer for our family and he thanked God for giving us thirteen and a half years with Neo. In closing, he told Neo goodnight, just as he did every night, when we heard the clicking of Neo walking down the hall to the side of Patrick's bed. Neo's nails were a little longer than usual just before his passing and you could always hear him coming as his nails made a clunking sound on the hardwood floors. He jumped up and said, "Did you hear that! I heard Neo!" I did hear it, it was emotional. To this very day, Neo seems to come around when Patrick needs him. He was always beside Patrick in life, so it didn't surprise me that he would be by his side after his passing. Patrick always said he would never get another dog after Neo and he was pretty firm on that. I can't say I blamed him. No dog could ever replace Neo.

A few months after losing Neo, Patrick was at work, he worked for the Parks Board doing landscaping and keeping the parks clean for everyone to enjoy. On one July day, it was very hot and humid when this Pitbull walked out from the woods towards Patrick, he froze in his tracks, because Pitbull's have a bad reputation for being aggressive. The dog got into his golf cart and started to lick on his water bottle. After Patrick realized he was thirsty and could tell by the ribs showing through his fur, this poor pup was starving. So, he opened his water bottle and let him drink the whole thing. The dog jumped up on his seat right next to him as Patrick was getting ready to leave and took a ride with him through the park. He took a video of them driving together in the golf cart and sent it to me. I knew at that very moment that Neo sent this dog to him. I told him that if he goes to the pound he will probably be put down because the SPCA is overloaded with Pitbull's. As soon as he put the video on social media, his page lit up with everyone telling him Neo sent this pup to him.

Patrick had to call the SPCA to come pick up the dog because he couldn't let him go back into the woods and starve to death. Once they came and took him away, Patrick couldn't shake him, he was on his mind all day. When he got off work, he decided to go see him at the SPCA. When he got home, he was telling me how he couldn't shake the feeling of this dog but said he just wasn't ready for another dog. Neo had just passed a few months prior and the wounds were still too raw.

The next few days after work, Patrick found himself going to the SPCA every day to see if he was still there, when finally, the lady at the SPCA said to him, "Do you want him? Why don't you just take him home, you obviously care about him and he only gets excited when you show up!"

Patrick went home and picked up Zian, Stewie and, Fenway and took them to the SPCA so they could all meet. The pup was so friendly, and they all got along, and the next thing I knew, Patrick was sending me a picture of Zian holding this Pitbull in his lap in the car. They were bringing Dude home. Yep, we named him Dude and it fits his personality perfectly. I couldn't wait to get home from work to meet Dude, I was showing everyone at work his picture like I just had another kid, I was so excited.

I was recently on a crime scene where a Pitbull mauled a little girl and another scene where a Pitbull killed his owner by mauling her to death, but these Pitbull's were treated badly and that's why they were aggressive. We didn't know Dude's past, so that worried me a bit.

Now you think we would have learned from Fenway and the cat debacle we had, but yet again it slipped our minds and we were right back in an episode of Tom and Jerry. At least it was only one cat instead of two that we would have to concentrate on since Teall had moved into her own apartment and took Church with her. At least Dude didn't take as long as Fenway, since we learned from our mistakes the first time. Dude fitted in perfectly. My heart was full, he was going to be a great addition to our family. Although Patrick doesn't believe it, we all still think Neo sent Dude to him, he will never take his place but this dog silly happy go lucky behavior just makes us laugh. He is the silliest dog I have ever owned. He is also needy and clingy like a dryer sheet you just can't seem to shake off your pants leg.

There are still days that Neo will pop in and let Patrick know that he is still watching over him, like the day Patrick was napping after work and he felt the bed go down like it would when Neo would get in bed with him. When he turned over to look, there was no one or nothing there. We still hear him clunking down the hallway at night.

One day I would get a call from Teall, she told me there is something wrong with her cat, Church. I went over to pick her up so we could take her to the vet. Unfortunately, there was nothing they could do for Church and Teall had to make the decision to let her go. We have lost so many pets in the last few years that it just hits you in your soul. It crushed me to see Teall sobbing and saying her goodbyes, just as we watched Zian do the same thing over Indy and Jr. She had 18 wonderful years with Church, and we are grateful for that. Church was also raised in our house for seventeen of those eighteen years she had on this earth, so it was in the back of my mind if she too would make an appearance.

My suspicions would be confirmed one day when I was blow drying my hair and I looked over and saw Church sitting on the steps, watching me through the banister as she always did after I got out of the shower. She was solid, and I even said "Hi" to her when I realized I was talking to a ghost. When I looked back over, she was gone. I couldn't wait to tell Teall, and when I did, she told me that she thinks Church is visiting her as well, because one of her other cats constantly looks at the spot where Church always slept in Teall's apartment.

For some reason, seeing a beloved pet doesn't bother me, but seeing someone that you don't know leaves you with a very uneasy feeling. I think it's because, not only do you not know who they are, but you don't know what they want.

Zian now has his own place with his boyfriend (and now fiancé), but when Zian moved he left the desk behind that the little girl hides under. He said he didn't want her to follow him and felt it was best to leave the desk here. As much as we would have liked him to take the desk, we understood why he didn't want it. We are now officially empty nesters.

After Patrick and I went on a cruise with our friends, we decided to remodel the first floor of our home, but we were weary because we both know when you change your home it can disrupt the spirits. We called our friend Taylor, she went to school with our daughter, and she also has abilities. We wanted to see if she knew anyone that could come over to our house before we do the remodel. She put my husband in contact with Lee and Patti, from a paranormal group she knows. Lee and Patti, field investigations for a major cable network, and if they find anything good, they have a TV crew come into the home for filming.

We set up a date and time for them to come to the house to see if they could find anything here. They told us they would be inviting their friend Jim over to the house because he is a medium, and he could read our place before the investigation. They told us, they just let Jim know there is a job at a certain time, but they don't give him the address until they arrive at the location. This way Jim has no idea where he is going until he gets the call and punches the address into his GPS, because in the days of computers you could research a house and get the names of a previous owner. This way everything stays honest.

When we contacted Lee and Patti, they didn't want to hear anything about what was going on in the house. They didn't want to know what the hot spots were or any of the activity we had experienced. Our friend Lee Ann was also at our house because she had experienced a lot of activity as well, so we wanted her to be a part of this investigation. Once they got to the house, they called Jim. While they waited for Jim, they started to get their equipment ready.

Once Jim arrived at our house, we all introduced ourselves and he explained that as he is reading the house, he doesn't want us to show a reaction if he is picking up on something. He didn't want us to confirm or deny anything he may be picking up on. I thought that was brilliant, because no one knew the activity we have encountered in the house. I have to say, I'm leery about anyone that calls themselves a medium until they prove it to me, like Jenny did at the Oakland house, and my cousin Nick.

The walk-through with Jim hadn't even started yet when he saw our shadow man standing in the dining room. He told us he saw a tall man with a hat on and as he walked into the dining room where he saw him, he said the energy was very high. He walked into the kitchen and looked up the steps where the kid's rooms were and stated he wanted to go up there next. As he went up the step, without hesitation he went into Zian's room, he walked across the room and turned to the desk and said, "There is a little girl hiding under the desk. Maybe four or five years old, but she is scared of the man in the house." Now how in the world are we supposed to contain ourselves. You walk in the room and say there is a little girl under the desk and we're not supposed to react? Are you freaking kidding me right now? When he turned his back to us, I just grabbed Lee Ann's and Patrick's arms and mouthed the words, "Can you believe this?" He then walks over to the attic crawl space and says, "She just went into the attic, she likes to hide in here too." which made total sense to us, because Zian said he would hear knocking in there.

From there he headed back down the steps and stopped about halfway and said there was something important about the steps but he wasn't quite sure what yet. He continued down the steps and looked out the backdoor and said he wanted to go out there later. He continued around the hallway and went into our room and stated he felt the man moving about the house more and into our bedroom. Great! That's just what a woman wants to hear. Anyway, he left our room and went down to the basement, he turned his head toward our washer and dryer and said, "Ohhhhh, he is an honorary one, isn't he?!" Ok, now I just want to go over and grab Jim by his shoulder and just shake him, and say "YES! YES! He is an honorary one, he flipped my clothes basket right HERE! He threw my loaf of bread onto the kitchen floor!" but as hard as it was, I kept my cool. He then told us this man had an attitude, that everything needed to be done now, right now, which was part of what was causing our anxiety, and he liked to be left alone, but he also liked to make his presence known in a mischievous way.

Jim headed back upstairs and back into our living room, he pointed to the side door leading out to our side porch where the hot tub sat and said, "Can I go out there?" We opened the door for him, he stepped out, and looked up over to the house next door and said he sensed an evil presence over there, but it was stuck in that house. He points up to the porch where Patrick and I had seen the shadow man on two separate occasions, and said he is stuck up there. He looked into our backyard and said there is a lot of energy inside and outside of the house. He wasn't sure if the man he saw in our house was attached to the house or the land. He felt like it was more the land that the house sat on. He also felt the little girl died close to our property, but not on this site, nor in this house. She attached to Zian because it felt safe to her, and that made us all sad.

Once he was finished with the walk-through, we told Lee, Patti, and Jim that he hit the mark on everything. We told them about the little girl Zian has seen in his room, and that she always hides under the desk, and how my cousin Nick saw the tall man standing in the dining room just as Jim did. I told him Zian left the desk here just for that very reason, he didn't want the little girl to follow him. I let Jim know I wanted to shake him when he was in the basement because he was blowing my mind. We all talked about our experiences and shared some video's we had of the activity.

Now it was Lee and Patti's turn to break out their high-tech equipment and head to Zian's room to investigate the hot spot in the house, if you will. Lee Ann and I sat closest to the bedroom door, Patrick was sitting on the floor right next to the desk, Jim was sitting on the floor next to the attic door while Lee and Patti were standing by the window, which was opposite Patrick.

The first thing they did was to put the Rem-Pod out, which is a proximity detector. If any spirit gets next to the small antenna sticking out of the top of the Rem-Pod, a light will flash and make a noise. When they set it on the floor it was sitting in front of Jim. Jim asked the little girl to come out and touch the toy they had sitting on the floor so she could see the shiny light. A few seconds after he said that the light went off for about 3 seconds and then stopped. He told her she did good and asked her to do it again, but then Jim said she is scared. The tall man is upstairs now, and she is afraid of him, so she won't come out of the attic. Lee and Patti were seeing orbs in the room on their video camera and I felt a cold spot in-between Lee Ann and I, she felt it too. Lee told us he saw an orb go in our direction. Patrick then started to get emotional and was crying, Lee took out the SLS (Structured Light Sensor) camera. As Patrick lay down on the floor, and he put his hand up and asked the little girl to touch his hand, and Lee said there was a stick figure showing in the SLS camera, sitting on the chair next to the desk, touching Patrick's hand. Patrick could feel the cold mass around his hand and then it just disappeared. At this time Jim said he wasn't feeling well, and the energy was starting to drain him.

I want to explain what an SLS camera is, it uses an RGB (Red, Green and Blue lights) camera with a depth sensor and infrared light projector. It can recognize people as a stick figure, and it can also recognize a spirit that cannot be seen by the naked eye, and project it onto the camera screen as a stick figure.

Patti and Lee decided to go into Teall's room while the rest of us stayed in Zian's room. We could hear them asking questions for an EVP session. This is simply using a voice recorder and asking questions while you leave a pause in between the questions to see if you get a response. At one point, Patti asked if the spirit could hit the drum set and make a noise. Upon playing it back it said, "I will not!" Lee then asked the spirit what his name was, and it said, "Leonard." Lee asked that question multiple times and always got the same response. They then ask why he make so much noise, when it responded, "I don't like stupid people."

Well, I can only imagine how many times we have pissed off "Leonard" with all of the pranks we play. Especially when Patrick filled my blow dryer with baby powder, so when I turned it on, I would get a face full of white powder, but instead, I held the dryer upward when the powder went up in the air, and my dryer caught on fire, setting off all of the smoke detectors in the house. No wonder "Leonard" is so angry, because between our pranks on one another, he must think we are pretty stupid. Nothing like a ghost in your house that doesn't have a sense of humor. You think after twenty years, he would have gotten used to us by now.

When we finally finished up, we told them that we planned to remodel the house, but we were afraid the activity would pick up. Jim told us we shouldn't fear what is here and that he may be grumpy, but he was not harmful. They told us to sage the house before we start construction and let "Leonard" know that we are just trying to improve the house for the better. Let them know they are welcome to stay, if they can learn their boundaries and know this is our house now.

Jim left, because as I said earlier the spirits were draining his energy and he wasn't feeling well, but Lee and Patti were excited about what they had caught and wanted to know if they could send a camera crew out, if they were interested in doing a show. I wasn't really sure how I felt about that because I'm afraid it would really upset "Leonard" and the activity could get worse.

The next month we were scheduled for our remodel, so Patrick and I saged the house again. We encouraged the little girl and Leonard to go to the light and said the prayer that we did the last time. The activity seemed to stop, so we went ahead and had the remodel begin the next month.

As the construction was getting underway, Covid-19 would put the entire country on lockdown, but luckily my brother-n-law was a contractor, and that's who we hired to do the job. My husband would lose his job for the next few months, but I was considered an essential worker, so we lucked out that we both didn't lose our jobs. The construction would last a couple of months, and things were still quiet, but we were worried that the door "Leonard" would go out when he came down the steps, if he was still even here, would upset him when we took out the door and made it into a wall, making our kitchen larger. We put a sliding glass door in the dining room where our window used to be so we would have better access to our deck, and oh yeah, we knocked out the wall between our kitchen and dining room, and put a bar there to make it an open concept. So, there were huge changes made to the entire first floor. Every room was repainted, and new flooring was put down on the entire first floor. We also knocked down the archway that "Leonard" liked to stand under between our living room and dining room. So yeah, we were very nervous, that if he stuck around, he would wreak havoc.

We would be free of activity for the summer, but then one night I was sitting on the couch and out of the corner of my eye, I saw a man dressed in a tan tweed suit with a hat on going out the new sliding glass door. When I looked over, he was gone. This is the first time in the house that I saw "Leonard" as a solid apparition. He has always been a shadow. I was shaking to my core. I thought we were finished with this, I thought they had left. The loud noises upstairs would start again, both Patrick and I would hear them, and one day we were watching TV together, it just turned off. I yelled, "Turn that back on, we were watching that!" Patrick asked me who I was talking to, I said, "Leonard! He needs to turn the TV back on." Just then the TV came back on, and I replied with a "Thank you!" I have to admit, I was shocked, but I played it cool and calm and just went about what I was doing.

One of the next big incidents would be when Teall was visiting. Patrick had just hung up one of my pictures in the dining room a few days earlier, and while Teall was looking at it and complimenting on how good it looked, it fell off the wall, and this square picture rolled two times behind my desk. We just looked at each other with both of our eyes ready to pop out of our heads. She asked if "Leonard" did that, so I checked the picture frame to see if the tape holding it wasn't strong enough. I told her I thought maybe it just wasn't put up with strong enough wall hangers, so I put one up that had an actual hook on it, and put the picture back on the wall. As I turned away from the picture I said, "If it falls again, then it's Leonard!" and before I could finish my sentence it fell off the wall again and the hook was still on the wall. This was the first thing Teall had ever witnessed with her own eyes. The look on her face was priceless though. When Patrick got home, he saw the picture leaning against the wall, and after we told him what had happened, he nailed it to the wall and said, "If he can get that off, more power to him." Fortunately, it stayed on the wall.

After that, Lee Ann and I decided to have a girl's night at my house. We sat by the firepit, had some drinks with a few laughs, and topped off the night sitting in the hot tub with a nightcap. Lee Ann retired to the couch, and I went to bed. When I got up the next morning, she looked exhausted. When I asked her how she slept, she said she didn't sleep at all because our ghosts kept her up all night chattering. She said there were two voices, but she couldn't make out what they were saying. She said this went on all night, along with the footsteps up in Zian's room.

Later that day, Patrick and I were watching some motorcycle racing when Dude stood up on the couch between us, he stepped over Patrick, with his two front paws on the armrest, hair raised on his back, he cocked his head sideways, ears propped up, and started growling at the desk in our dining room; where the picture that fell off the wall hangs. Patrick paused the racing on the TV, and we both leaned forward slowly looking into the dining room and saw the horse statue that I bought for my dad when I was a kid, rocking back and forth. There are three horses on one end, and then there is a ten-inch wire with a weighted ball on the other end, and in the center, there is a point that sits on top of a stand, and if you push it, it will go in a complete circle making the three horses look like they're galloping. Well, the horses were bouncing up and down, and it has never done that before. We have the old radiator heaters and no vented air, so there was nothing to make the horses move. It had sat in the same spot for five years since my dad passed away, and never moved.

    To date, the activity is probably at the highest it has ever been. The only thing I can think of that made the activity spike again, was the party my neighbor Fran had. She had an all-female party with about thirty women there, and somehow, we got on the subject of ghosts, and I told them my story. Lee Ann and I were going to run down to my house and grab a few beers when one of the girls asked if she could come with us. When we got to my house, she wanted to go up in Zian's room, so we took her up there. The next thing I knew, two more girls from the party showed up to my house, one being Ann that lives three doors up from me, that also has activity in her home. Ann had the same feeling Patrick did in Zian's room when the paranormal team was at our house. She felt overwhelmed with sadness, so I decided it probably wasn't a good idea to have so many people up there that claimed to be sensitive too. I think maybe "Leonard" kept up his end of the bargain, but by me bringing these women upstairs, I broke our end of the deal. After everyone left, Lee Ann crashed on the couch and was kept up all night by the banging and footsteps coming from upstairs. This all happened prior to the picture incident, Dude growling, and Lee Ann hearing the chattering, as she crashes here on occasion since her husband is an over the road truck driver.

    What concerns me is that Patrick and I are going to remodel the entire upstairs, "Leonard's" and the little girl's safe space. I'm worried about what's to come. If 2020 wasn't a crazy enough year, it scares me to think what 2021 could bring when we begin our renovations up there.

I have spent hours at the Historical Society in my town, and no one by the name of Leonard has owned this home since it was built in 1959. We are the longest to ever live in this home which makes me question, have others that lived here had the same experiences we have? It really makes me think about when we bought this house and we offered them $20,000 less than they were asking, because it was out of our budget. They were too quick to take our offer, and that should have been a sign to us, but we were just happy to have landed this house with a huge backyard for our children and dogs. I still don't have any solid answers as to who "Leonard" is, but I did find a map from 1865, and an L. Williams owned the property butting up to where our house now sits. Unfortunately, those maps only give initials with last names, but I would really love to know what the "L" stands for in front of the name Williams.

    I am still researching, but for now, I guess we'll all have to wait to see what is in store for us when we start the renovations upstairs. We have been in contact with Lee and his team and they are going to do more investigating once Covid takes a back seat and restrictions are lifted, but for now, this is where my story ends.

## Final Thoughts

For me, I have more questions than answers. Like, why is our family so prone to paranormal activity? Are we sensitive? Are we just so open and attract spirits? Does it run in our family, and since Patrick and I are sensitive, Zian was then born with the gift more powerful than our own? Why doesn't Teall see what we see, is it because Jenny had me sit outside while they cleansed the "Oakland" house while I was pregnant with her?

I do believe that when we are born our lives are already paved for us, and the experiences we have from birth, and throughout our lives, are laying the foundation. It's like we are being prepped for our future, but some people may go their whole lives not understanding what is being laid out right in front of them. For example, when I was a teenager, I was terrified of death. Were these experiences paving the way for me to become a Crime Scene Investigator? If you would have told me this was going to be my profession back then, I would have laughed at you.

Numbers also have me baffled. For as long as man has walked this earth they have been obsessed with numbers and what they represent, like "13" and "666". I have three sets of numbers that represent something for me and always seem to show up when I need comforting or when I'm thinking about a specific person. I have to say "286", my badge number, has been a very important number to me before I ever knew it. When my mom brought her and dad's plots in the cemetery back when I was a teenager, and my dad's plot number would end up being "286" still has my mind blown. At that time in my life, I hadn't thought about being a police officer anymore like I did when I was a child, because so many deaths had impacted me back then, that I never gave it another thought until I had children of my own, and then that dream was refreshed in me. Not only was "286" my badge number, but it would end up being the beginning of our son's SOC number. When you think about all of the numbers he could have been assigned at birth, all of the badge numbers I could have been given, and of all of the plot numbers my dad could have been assigned, will make one's head spin.

Another thing that has my head spinning is my dreams. The first as a child, that I had hundreds of times and then stopped once I fell down the steps. The dream with my aunt giving me a warning that I would lose someone very special to me. I could go on and on. I am no closer to understanding why these things happen to me, but when I wake up and I can remember a vivid dream, it sometimes terrifies me.

There are so many people in my life that have made an impact on me. My Poppy was one of those people, so I thought it was fitting to use his painting he made when he was 96 yrs. old as the cover on my book.

Made in the USA
Monee, IL
15 May 2022